DEDICATION

To my three beautiful children and their wonderful spouses.
What a gift and delight each of you are.

Every time I think of you, I give thanks to my God.

—Philippians 1:3

ACKNOWLEDGMENTS

I'm so thankful for:

Jesus. My Savior, Redeemer, and Friend.

My husband and family. Your steadfast love and support bring me so much joy.

My critique group. Thank you, ladies, for pouring into me week after week. I love the laughs, learning, and accountability we share.

My agent. Tamela Hancock Murray, your patience and wisdom have blessed me in so many ways.

The team at Iron Stream Media. I appreciate Susan Cornell, Michele Trumble, Kim McCulla, and the wonderful editors you've brought on board—Ann Tatlock, I'm looking at you—for making the book shine. What a privilege it is to work with you.

My readers. Thank you for all the ways you inspire me. It's an honor and blessing to share my stories with you. Keep in touch by visiting me at my website, www.nancylavo.com.

"Author Nancy Lavo had me heart and soul with this endearing story of love, purpose, and the desires of our hearts. A cast of memorable characters brings this book to life while Lavo weaves in faith elements and spiritual truth with a masterful touch. A pure delight! I can't wait to read more from this author."

—**Lori Altebaumer**, author of *Beneath the Broken Oak*

"Sweet and funny and poignant and a host of other good things. Lavo has covered all the bases in *Heart and Soul*, a story of love and faith and sacrifice—a sigh-inducing, can't-help-but-smile read that will melt your heart. Five stars!"

—**Lori DeJong**, award-winning author of the True Calling series

"In *Heart and Soul*, Nancy Lavo proves she's the undisputed queen of Christian romantic comedy. This funny, heartwarming story hits on all levels!"

—**Teresa Wells**, author of *What Brings Us Joy*

"Nancy Lavo's *Heart and Soul*, book four in the Lone Star Loves series, sizzles in the purest way—like hot kettle corn syrup, rich with sweetness and just enough heat to keep your heart racing. With faith woven into every page and a romance that glows with God-honoring passion, this story is a tender triumph. Lavo delivers relatable characters, palpable chemistry, and a love that lingers long after you turn the last page."

—**Cindee Appling**, award-winning author

LONE STAR LOVES

Heart and Soul

BOOK 4

NANCY LAVO

Birmingham, Alabama

Heart and Soul

Iron Stream Fiction
An imprint of Iron Stream Media
100 Missionary Ridge
Birmingham, AL 35242
IronStreamMedia.com

Library of Congress Control Number: 2025932720

Scripture quotations are taken from the Holy Bible, New Living Translation, copyright ©1996, 2004, 2015 by Tyndale House Foundation. Used by permission of Tyndale House Publishers, Carol Stream, Illinois 60188. All rights reserved.

Cover design by For the Muse Designs

ISBN: 978-1-56309-786-7 (paperback)
ISBN: 978-1-56309-787-4 (eBook)

1 2 3 4 5—29 28 27 26 25

CHAPTER ONE

The day only needed this.

Noah Speers eased his Tesla to the side of the street, lights from the police car strobing in his rearview mirror. Several cars cruised past, eager witnesses to his humiliation, while the cop climbed from his vehicle and approached.

Noah powered down the window and was greeted with a blast of hot August air. "Is there a problem, officer?"

The cop leaned in. "Nice ride." He made a point of looking Noah over before turning his gaze to the computer screen that served as a dashboard. "Will it operate at thirty miles an hour? I only ask because that's the speed limit our fair city has designated for this stretch of road." He pointed in the direction Noah had just come from. "You may have noticed the sign."

Okay, Lord, I probably deserved this. But did You have to send a smart aleck? No matter. He could talk his way out of trouble with this backwoods Barney. Noah flashed a toothy smile. "You probably don't recognize me."

"Can't say that I do. License and registration, please."

"I do a lot of interviews on Christian television." He tipped down his mirrored sunglasses. Another smile. More teeth. "Noah Speers?"

The cop spared him a cursory glance. "Not ringing a bell."

"I'm in town to help out at the church while the pastor is incapacitated." Even the hardest-nosed law enforcement wasn't likely to ticket a man on a mission of mercy. He dug his wallet from his back pocket and handed his license through the window, then reached into the glove compartment for his registration. "Are you acquainted with Dale Willbanks?"

"Sure. Everybody knows Pastor Dale." The cop gave Noah a skeptical once-over. "You're a preacher?"

Noah nodded. "From Houston. You've heard of Celebration Fellowship, I'm sure."

"Nope."

Further proof he'd traveled beyond the edge of civilization. "It's my father's church. Actually, my grandfather started it. Counting satellites, we've got fifty thousand members."

That got the yahoo's attention. His eyes widened as he let out a low whistle. "Dang. I bet your potlucks are amazing."

"Potlucks? Oh. Ha ha." Small-town humor. This guy was a regular laugh riot. "I'm the associate executive pastor on the main campus."

Another whistle. "Sounds like an important job. Surprised they can spare you."

If that was sarcasm he heard in the cop's voice, he chose to ignore it. "I won't be here for long." *Please, God.* "Just a couple of days."

"I see." The cop handed back the license and registration. "Since Pastor Dale is a good friend, I'm going to let you off with a warning. But while you're staying in Village Green, I expect you to obey the speed limits, hotshot associate executive pastor or not."

Noah tamped down his irritation, resisted a snarky comeback or an eye roll. Hardly an appropriate response for a man of God. Even a cranky one.

"Thank you, Officer . . ."—he glanced at the name tag on his uniform—"Walker. I'll do that."

"'Spect I'll see you in church on Sunday." The cop rapped the glass roof of the car before stepping back. "Good to meet you, Hotshot."

"Noah." He leaned out the window to call after him. "It's Noah."

He started the engine, closed the window of his now-sweltering car, and pulled out behind a slow-moving pickup truck into the light traffic. According to the app, he had less than two miles to his destination.

Despite the hokey slogan painted on the sign at the edge of town, the little bit of Village Green he'd seen confirmed this was not the place for him. Noah Speers was a big-city guy with a preference for new and shiny. Antiquated towns with empty sidewalks and dreary brick buildings depressed him. He liked glass-and-steel high-rises, bustling traffic, and the noise of activity.

He didn't do quaint.

Maybe his attitude would be better if he understood why he was here. Why had his healthy grandfather insisted Noah leave his comfortable home and busy job to help out his old crony from seminary days when he could easily do the job himself? It didn't make sense. The visit would have given the old guys an excuse to rehash stories from their nearly sixty years of friendship.

Noah had agreed, of course. He'd do anything for his family. But he wasn't happy about it. And the long drive from Houston had given him hours to brood over the inconvenience and waste of his time.

Dismay mixed with a sense of ill-usage when, minutes later, he pulled up to the address he'd been given. His grandfather had explained his friend Dale lived in a parsonage, but Noah had assumed that meant a home in keeping with the position of head pastor. This parsonage was little bigger than a dollhouse.

At least the wood-frame home appeared to be well maintained, the paint fresh and landscaping neat. It was just so . . . tiny. The entire structure would fit inside his parents' entry hall.

And he was supposed to share this with a complete stranger? A worse thought struck him. Would they be bunking in the same room?

Lord, You've made a terrible mistake.

An old man with a shock of white hair hobbled out onto the front porch and waved in his direction.

Duty called. With a huff of resignation, Noah climbed out of the car and returned the wave. He crossed the lawn and took the short flight of stairs two at a time.

"Hello." He extended his hand to the man. "I'm Noah Speers. You must be Dale Willbanks."

"I am." The old man took the proffered hand in a surprisingly strong grip. "Welcome." He studied Noah openly. "You've got the look of your grandfather."

"Thank you, sir. I take that as a compliment." Like his grandfather, Noah's host appeared to be every bit of eighty. "He sends his regards."

"I was sorry to hear about your grandmother's passing, Noah. Susan was a lovely woman. Your grandfather and Susan and my wife, Betty, and I spent many happy hours together in seminary." He chuckled. "We were so poor, the only entertainment we could afford was playing cards or board games. We got to know one another very well."

"My grandfather still talks about the fun you four had back in the day."

The light in the older man's bright blue eyes dimmed and his smile faded as he looked beyond Noah's shoulder to some unseen point. "My Betty passed away ten years ago. I miss her every day." After a moment's pause, he faced Noah. "Your grandfather and I were blessed in our helpmates. A pastor's wife is critical to his ministry."

He didn't know if the old guy spoke in generalities or if he directed his remark specifically to Noah's single state. "Yes, sir."

"Enough reminiscing." Dale smiled broadly as he clapped him on the back. "Come in the house. We can get your suitcase later. There's someone I'd like you to meet."

Noah expected some sort of welcome delegation, perhaps the lay leadership of the church coming by to express their gratitude. Somebody had better appreciate what he was doing. He smoothed the creases in his slacks and patted his fingers across his hair as he followed Dale inside.

As his vision adapted to the shadowy interior, he was relieved to discover the house was pleasant, even cozy, in a miniaturized sort of way. Walls painted in light colors and comfortable furnishings in shades of green and tan lent it a homey atmosphere. Dale led him through a small living room to the equally small kitchen and extended a hand toward a dark-haired woman seated at a round table.

"Dr. Emily Cutler, I'd like you to meet Noah Speers." Dale turned to Noah. "Emily is also new to Village Green, just setting up her practice. I invited her to dinner before I knew you were coming, but I believe your arriving here tonight is providential. You've saved this bright young woman from the drudgery of making conversation with an old man."

"Talking with you is anything but drudgery," Emily replied before standing to shake Noah's hand. She was so short, the top of her head was even with his shoulder. "I passed you on my drive here. The police had you pulled over."

Noah gave her a tight smile. "Nice of you to mention it."

"Bless your heart." She had the nerve to laugh. "Trouble with the law on your first day in town." She shook her head. "Not an auspicious beginning."

"Oh, dear." At least the old man had the decency to look sympathetic. "I hope you didn't get a ticket."

"No, sir. I confess I invoked your name, and he let me off with a warning."

The doctor continued to chuckle over his misfortune. If this was his welcoming committee, she left much to be desired.

An awful thought occurred to him. Was she here because Dale was trying his age-spotted hand at matchmaking? Hadn't he just told Noah how important a wife was to the ministry?

He gave the thirtyish woman another look. *No, thanks.* Noah Speers didn't need any help with the fairer sex. And even if he did, Dr. Emily Cutler wasn't his type.

Born and raised in Houston, he'd been surrounded by beautiful women his whole life—stylish, polished women who knew from birth how to employ a myriad of tools to enhance their natural beauty. When it was time to marry, in the far distant future, he would turn to one of those.

This pint-sized person—with her thick brows and straight, dark hair parted in the middle and hanging in a fat braid down to who-knew-where—had zero style. And no polish. None. He studied her more closely. And not a drop of makeup. Within his broad circle of acquaintances, he didn't know a single woman over the age of thirteen who didn't use at least some cosmetics.

Maybe she shunned outer adornment to focus on inner beauty. That would explain the frumpy clothes. If so, more power to her.

Although he didn't think people with inner beauty made a habit of enjoying other people's troubles.

To be fair, Emily of the importunate amusement had nice eyes. Big and blue, several shades darker than his host's, and framed with thick lashes, they spoke of vitality and intelligence. And mirth.

Whatever. Though not precisely a troll, the doctor was definitely not his type.

Emily stared up at six feet of male perfection. She'd seen good-looking men before, but this guy occupied a league all his own. Wavy blond hair, not a strand out of place, chiseled features glossed with a healthy tan, broad shoulders on a lean muscular frame tapering to a narrow waist—he had it all.

Which only made her more aware of her own shortcomings.

And when she felt self-conscious, she laughed.

Painful experience had taught her that trying to squelch the laughter didn't work. Suppressing nature's way of releasing pent-up emotion would lead to raucous guffaws or, worse, barnyard snorts.

Not the way to make a good first impression.

She had no choice but to ride it out. So, she continued to laugh, thankfully now downgraded to a chuckle, in the face of his obvious irritation.

Smiling, Dale looked from one to the other. "Before I wrenched my back, I'd planned on burgers tonight. If one of you doesn't mind taking over the grill for me, I think we can make this work."

Emily waited a beat for Noah to volunteer for the typically male domain. When his offer wasn't forthcoming, she made it for him. "Noah can handle the burgers, and I'll take the inside prep. Dale, you can sit down and act as manager."

Dale must have noticed Noah's silence. "What do you say, Noah? Are you up for head chef tonight?"

"Yes, sir." He wrung his hands. "Happy to. You'll have to direct me—"

"The grill's out there." He pointed to the sliding glass door behind the kitchen table. "The charcoal, lighter fluid, and matches are in a green plastic tub on the edge of the patio."

Noah paused, lips parted, as if to say something. Then, apparently deciding against it, he moved to the sliding glass door and walked outside.

Dale stepped farther into the kitchen. "Let me get the ground meat from the refrigerator and get started on the patties."

Emily shook her head. "Oh no you don't. You sit and keep me company while I make them."

He frowned. "I hate to be useless."

She stood and pointed him toward her now-vacant chair. "You're not useless, just working in an advisory capacity until that back heals up. How is it?"

"Better today, thanks to you." He lowered himself gingerly into the seat. "I've been using the heating pad and taking the ibuprofen like you told me to."

She cupped a hand to her ear. "*Ahh*, the sound of patient compliance. Such a rare and beautiful music to a doctor's ears."

He laughed. "Pastors and doctors have that in common. We can give people the answers, but until they're willing to apply them, things don't get better."

She smiled, grateful to have someone who understood. "Exactly. They warned us in medical school about the extremely low percentage of patients who actually complete the prescribed course of action, but it still frustrates me. What good does it do to offer the solutions if people refuse to use them?" She washed her hands at the sink before pulling the meat from the refrigerator. "It never occurred to me that pastors face the same frustration."

"Sad fact of life. People want the answers until they realize it requires some effort on their part." He bobbed his head in commis-eration. "When you're ready, the platters are in the cabinet to the left. Salt and pepper by the stove."

She turned to face him. "And the Worcestershire sauce?"

He grinned. "I see you're a woman who knows her way around a burger. It's on the door of the fridge. Right side."

"I'm the oldest of four children." She shook the Worcestershire into the meat and blended it in with her hands. "My parents worked late, so we all had to learn to cook. Most of the time, the responsibil-ity fell to me. Luckily, I enjoy it."

As she formed the patties, she glanced through the glass door to see how Noah was progressing with the fire. He wasn't. The red metal grill stood untouched at the edge of the concrete patio while he held the charcoal bag at eye level and away from his pristine white shirt, turning it from side to side as though he were looking for something.

She finished the last patty, placed it on the platter with the others and, after washing her hands again, returned them to the refrigerator.

"I'm going to check how things are going outside," she told Dale. "Be right back."

Noah looked up as she slid open the door, a wary expression on his handsome face. Poor man was probably waiting for her to laugh.

"Everything okay out here?"

"Yeah. Sure." He returned his attention to the bag. "Just looking for the instructions."

Instructions? To start a grill fire? As she stepped out onto the patio and closed the door behind her, she remembered her early years in medical school and residency, when the older students and doctors mocked the younger interns and residents for their lack of knowledge. Though regarded as harmless hazing, a rite of passage, she'd always felt it was cruel and demeaning. Having felt the sting of their derision, she'd sworn she'd never ridicule anyone for their ignorance.

"I bet you're a gas grill kind of guy." She walked over to him. "I should have asked before I volunteered you for the job."

She removed the rack from the grill and pointed to the well in the center. "Go ahead and dump in about a third of the bag."

He tipped the bag, funneling a heap of black briquettes into the grill and hopping back as a cloud of black dust billowed out.

"Now, we'll stack them like this." She adopted an instructional tone as she built a medium-sized pyramid. When she finished, she reached toward him. "Lighter fluid."

He handed her the plastic bottle and a box of matches. She squeezed on a generous squirt. Careful not to touch him with her filthy fingers, she waved him to a safe distance. "Stand back."

She struck a match and tossed it onto the pile. It flamed up with a gratifying whoosh. "Voilà."

Smiling, she turned to him. Instead of sharing her delight over her very nice fire, he regarded her from beneath furrowed brows in the same way she would look at mysterious bacteria on a slide under a microscope.

Uh-oh. She felt the laughter building, rising like tiny bubbles in her throat. She clapped a hand over her mouth. Too late. A merry snort escaped.

"We'll give the fire time to burn down, then I'll bring you the burgers." Her words were barely intelligible through the chortles.

With one last look at his beautiful, annoyed face, Emily ducked into the house.

*   *   *

The diminutive doctor had missed her calling. She should have been a comedienne.

Noah's phone vibrated, his father's name on the screen. He turned, putting his back to the kitchen door for privacy. "Hey, Dad. What's up?"

"Your mother was worried when we didn't hear from you. Did you make it to Village Green yet?"

"Yeah. Sorry I didn't call. As soon as I got here, they put me to work. At this very moment I'm preparing to grill hamburgers."

"You're a man of hidden talents. I didn't know you knew how."

"I don't. As soon as we get off the phone, I'll YouTube it."

"Good thinking. How's Dale?"

"We've haven't had a whole lot of time to talk, but he seems nice. I can't say the same for the girl."

"Girl?"

"Some doctor friend of his that he invited to dinner. He said he hadn't known I was coming when he asked her. I just hope this isn't some kind of matchmaking thing."

"Surely not. Is she pretty?"

Noah thought about her blue eyes. "She's not ugly. I'd be more inclined to like her if she stopped laughing at me."

"A woman laughing at you? Now that's a change. What does she find so funny?"

Noah sighed. "Apparently, it's hilarious I got stopped by the police on my way into town, and I imagine she's still laughing over the fact I didn't know how to start a charcoal fire."

"I'm sorry, Son. She sounds thoughtless."

"No worries. I won't be here long. And even in a Podunk town like this, I should be able to avoid one annoying woman for a couple of days."

"I just talked to Noah. He's miserable already."

Jim Speers, Noah's grandfather, laughed. "So?"

Noah's father, Paul, sighed. "So, I just don't see the need to punish him. Noah's a great kid, the best son a man could ask for."

Jim nodded. "He is a great guy. Nobody respects him more than me. And it's not punishment. We're just trying to broaden his horizons."

"Dad, he's been all over the world. He's only thirty years old and has already logged more miles than you and me together. I think his education is broad enough."

"Noah has seen the world as a first-class passenger. Before he's ready to take on a new role serving as teaching pastor, he needs to experience life in coach."

CHAPTER TWO

"M ove over."
Sunday morning, Noah glanced up from the screen of his phone to find Emily standing in the aisle beside his pew. He frowned. "Why?"

The doctor angled her head toward the back of the sanctuary. "Because Pastor Dale sent me up here to sit with you." She shrugged. "I guess he doesn't want you to be alone."

No way. He didn't need company. Especially not hers. He directed his attention back to his phone in pointed dismissal. "Thanks for the offer, but alone's good."

A moment later, he noted from the corner of his eye that she hadn't moved and, in fact, now made a scooting motion with her hands. "Move over," she repeated.

Noah frowned. He didn't want to cause a scene, and she wasn't giving up. Fine. He slid down the ancient pew, giving a wide berth to the human hyena.

And to think the day had started out so well.

His quiet time had been amazing. Last night he'd been relieved to discover that, although he'd be sharing a bathroom with Dale, at least each man had his own bedroom. Noah's cramped quarters didn't offer a desk or even a chair, so this morning he sat on the end of the surprisingly comfortable double bed to read and pray.

Spending his first hour with God, a habit he'd begun years ago, never failed to fill him with peace and joy. He loved God and His Word. As the psalmist said, God was his Rock, his Strength, and his Song.

This morning he'd had a breakthrough. For the last six months, he'd battled a building sense of frustration. He appreciated his job. Truly. He knew his current position in administration was temporary, like working his way from the mailroom up the corporate ladder. He understood the importance of knowledge about the many facets involved in leading a church. He acknowledged that by having him manage the day-to-day operations, his father and grandfather were preparing him for the future, and that even in the tedious job, he made a crucial contribution to the organization.

But he hated it.

He wanted to preach. He wanted to speak the Word he loved and share it in a life-giving way that changed hearts.

Noah had known from childhood that God had gifted him to preach and teach. He currently taught the singles group Bible study, and while he enjoyed it, he wanted to do more.

He'd spoken to his father and grandfather about it hundreds of times over the last few years, and each time they assured him they'd open the pulpit to him when he was ready. Nothing he said would convince them he was ready now.

So, he waited. Because he wasn't a patient man, every day of delay felt like a beating. Yet he didn't want to step out ahead of God, so he submitted—waiting and praying and trusting that God had not forgotten him and would show them all when the time was right.

He couldn't say he received a definitive start date, but this morning he'd sensed God's approval. At least he was on the right track.

When he finished the rich prayer time, he reviewed the sermon he'd prepared for this morning. He'd poured a lot of time into the brief message—a true labor of love. Having the opportunity to preach was the one bright spot in the trip.

Not knowing how much time they allotted the speaker, he tailored it to fifteen minutes. Short and to the point.

When he met Pastor Dale in the sunny kitchen over a breakfast of scrambled eggs and bacon, he was primed and ready to go.

Noah filled his coffee cup with the aromatic brew from the carafe on the table. "I'm excited about my sermon. I think you're really going to like it."

White brows furrowed, the older man lowered his cup. "Sermon?"

Nodding, he spooned several scoops of the eggs onto his plate. "Yes, sir. When my grandfather told me about your back injury and asked me to help out until you were feeling better, naturally I assumed you'd want me to preach. My text is—"

Dale shook his head. "I'm sorry, Noah. I'm afraid there's been a misunderstanding. I'm so grateful you're willing to help, but I've got a sermon already prepared. I'm doing a series on Corinthians, we're a couple weeks into it now, and I'd hate to lose the continuity."

"Oh." Noah's mood deflated like a two-day-old balloon. He'd been dragged to the middle of nowhere for nothing. "But what about your back?"

Another shake of the white head, this time accompanied with a smile. "Shouldn't be a problem. It's a bit unorthodox, but I'm going to preach sitting down. The custodian placed a chair by the pulpit. Dr. Emily says if I baby my back, the strain should clear up in no time."

"That's good to hear." Noah wasn't too sure how much credence he'd put in the merry medic's diagnosis, but the sooner Dale was healthy, the sooner he'd be out of there.

"Don't think that coming here was a waste of your time." Dale turned his wise blue eyes to him. "I could really use help with my home and hospital visits. Even before I pulled my back, I've had a terrible time getting in and out of the car. The doctor says I've got a touch of arthritis. Climbing in and out of the old Chevy is tough on these weary bones."

Home and hospital visits? Noah had never made one in his life. His father had a whole team of paid staff dedicated to pastoral care. Obviously, this church was smaller than his father's, but even the tiniest congregation didn't expect the head pastor to spend his time running from house to house, did they?

Noah pushed the question past reluctant lips. "So, how many visits do you make in a week?"

The old man put down his fork, tilting his head to calculate. "Eight or nine home visits and any hospital stops that come up. We don't have anyone sick right now, praise God."

Praise God, indeed. *And Lord, while You're at it, would you keep them healthy till I can make my escape?*

Frustration had heaped on frustration. Instead of using his gift, he'd be wasting time going door to door like a solicitor selling magazine subscriptions.

Noah glanced at the doctor from the corner of his eye. Now, to add insult to injury, here, in what should be the safety of the sanctuary, Dale stuck him with her. Again.

Noah didn't stop scooting until his hip bumped the far arm of the pew. Maybe she'd take the hint.

Emily continued to slide along the bench before settling in beside him, far enough away as befitting two near-strangers and close enough that he could hear her whispers. "Pretty church, isn't it?"

The remark didn't require an answer, so he ignored her. He wasn't interested in talking. Besides the church wasn't pretty so much as it was old. He spared a glance around the small sanctuary.

Lots of dark wood and stained glass windows. The tiny church looked old, smelled old, felt old.

"You can almost sense the history."

Turning, he looked at her then, trying to reconcile the fanciful statement with the woman he'd pegged as no-nonsense. She certainly looked no-nonsense with her unstylish white blouse tucked into an equally unstylish knee-skimming navy skirt. Today she reprised yesterday's hairstyle of a single braid down her back. Not a speck of makeup on her face.

She had pretty skin.

Noah looked away before she caught him staring. He didn't have to like her to notice she had a nice complexion. And just because he didn't care for her warped sense of humor, it didn't mean he couldn't appreciate her amazing eyes. Blue and clear like the deep waters of the Caribbean, and rimmed with thick, dark lashes, they demanded a second look.

Just then, an old woman—he was definitely seeing a pattern here—sat at the piano on the other side of the railing separating the altar from the rest of the sanctuary and began to play something slow and lumbering. Beside him, Emily grabbed a book from the rack built into the modesty partition and popped to her feet.

Ah. The praise and worship segment of the service. A sure remedy for his rotten mood. Noah stood and scanned the front of the sanctuary for projection screens. The congregation had completed the first line before he acknowledged there were no lyrics projected anywhere.

"I've got the page right here." Emily shifted the book, positioning it halfway between them.

The book, which he now recognized as an aged hymnal, presented each song as a sheet of music, the lyrics and notes on the same page. Which would be helpful except that, based on what he read, the pianist was making up her own tempo.

Instead of playing the prescribed lively allegro, she dragged along at adagio. Like a dirge.

The doctor must have noticed he wasn't singing because she lifted the book higher, presumably to make it easier for him to see.

With gentle pressure, he pushed it back toward her. "I'm not much of a singer."

She was so short he delivered the whispered remark to the top of her head. Apparently she heard, because she turned slightly to give him a smile of acknowledgment while continuing to sing in a beautiful alto.

No way he was opening his mouth. If she thought his brush with the law and grilling ineptitude were funny, his singing would send her into hysterics.

A skilled musician, he knew all too well he couldn't carry a tune. His own doting mother, the person most likely to find virtue in everything he did, once told him it didn't matter that he sang like a frog when he had so many other wonderful gifts.

The amphibian description was generous.

For years he'd petitioned the Almighty for a better voice. He didn't think he was being greedy—average skill would be fine—but so far the Lord had not granted his request. Noah believed God answered all prayer—yes, no, or later—so he continued to ask. A man of God, future leader of the largest church in the South, should be able to lead his flock in praise.

In the meantime, he'd keep his mouth shut and his secret safe.

Emily sat as the endless hymn finally dragged to a close. Beside her, Noah lowered himself to the pew, leaving a good foot and a half between them. Clearly, he hadn't warmed up to her company.

She wished she could tell him he wasn't the only one suffering.

How did he think she felt sitting next to him? Sharing a pew with human perfection was no picnic. It brought to mind an old fairy tale, with her cast as Beast to his Beauty. Every insecurity rose to the forefront of her mind.

She was too short. Too shy. Too plain.

As a little girl, her mother used to tell her God had given her a good heart and a good brain, and He expected her to use them for His glory. Just once she would have preferred to hear God made her as beautiful as a princess.

Over the years, her practical nature asserted itself. If kind and smart were the tools she'd gotten, then kind and smart was who she'd be. Pretty was overrated.

She glanced at Noah from the corner of her eye. Okay, a little pretty would be welcome just now. She wasn't asking to be a raving beauty. Mildly attractive would do. Just enough to make her feel less of a beast.

He dressed beautifully, if a tad formally for the casual gathering, in an expensive-looking light gray suit with a white shirt and blue tie. The whole ensemble fit so perfectly, it looked as though it were made for him.

She inhaled quietly. He even smelled beautiful. She'd noticed last night while standing beside him to stack charcoal that he smelled clean and sunny, like freshly washed sheets on the clothesline. When she tried to share a hymnal with him, she'd caught a whiff of the same light fragrance.

Emily hadn't worn perfume since . . . ever. When she was younger, she didn't have the money to purchase a fragrance, and now that she could afford it, she was too busy and too practical to waste time and resources on frivolous luxuries. Besides, perfume triggered allergies. She couldn't very well do that to her patients.

Pastor Dale stood and led them in prayer before taking the seat set up for him in front of the altar. He seemed to be moving more naturally this morning. If he'd follow her advice and take it easy for a week, he'd be back to his old, active self.

The man was a wonder. Eighty years old and still going strong. Though his body showed some signs of his advanced age, his mind remained young and sharp.

This Sunday marked her third week at the little country church, and she could honestly say she'd been looking forward to hearing the sermon all week. His previous teaching on Corinthians had been interesting and insightful. Dale possessed an encyclopedic knowledge of Scripture and tremendous skill at making the Word applicable to today. She pulled her journal and pen from her bag and settled back to listen.

Almost immediately she was drawn into his remarks. If it weren't for the constant bouncing of Noah's right knee, she'd have forgotten her pretty pew partner entirely. The thirty-minute sermon passed so quickly that when Dale bowed his head in a closing prayer, she glanced at her watch in surprise.

"We have a special guest with us this morning." Dale extended a hand toward their first-row pew. "Pastor Noah Speers is visiting here from Houston. His grandfather and I met at seminary nearly sixty years ago and have been dear friends ever since. When I mentioned my back problem to him, he suggested his grandson help us out while I'm recuperating. Noah has graciously agreed to join us and handle visitations till I'm feeling more spry."

Dale waited until the chatter died down before continuing. "Immediately following the service, we'll gather in the fellowship hall for our covered-dish luncheon, and you all will have the opportunity to meet him."

Emily bent to replace her journal in her bag. Big gatherings weren't her thing. While the others filed from the sanctuary to the fellowship hall, she'd make a discreet detour to the parking lot. Dale had sent her home last night with leftover burgers. She'd heat one of them up for her lunch.

After giving the benediction and dismissing the service, Dale stepped down from the platform and made a beeline to their pew. "Emily, I want you to sit with Noah and me at lunch. It'll be nice for him to have a familiar face at the table." He gave them a little wave, then proceeded down the aisle.

She turned to look up at Noah. "Why is it difficult for me to believe you have a problem with shyness?"

He grinned, the first genuine smile she'd received from him since they'd met. "Probably because I don't."

"I didn't think so." Of course not. The concept would be completely foreign to a man like him. She darted a look around. Half the congregation headed to a door in the front of the sanctuary to the right of the altar, while the remainder made their way to the back of the church where Pastor Dale was shaking hands. Maybe she could still slip out . . .

Noah leaned toward her. "I think the window for escape has closed," he whispered.

She frowned up into his handsome face. How did he know what she was thinking? Her shoulders sagged with resignation, and she sighed. "Yeah."

"Let me guess. You do have a problem with shyness, right?"

She straightened and lifted her chin. "I'm an introvert."

He shrugged. "Splitting hairs. I don't guess introverts like covered-dish lunches."

"Making endless small talk with a room full of strangers?" She grimaced. "I'd prefer open-heart surgery without anesthesia."

"That bad, huh?" To her surprise, he appeared genuinely concerned. "I'm sorry. I don't see any way out, especially since everyone heard Dale invite you to our table. It would look bad if you disappeared."

She'd come to the same conclusion.

"No problem. Stick with me and I'll run interference." He motioned for her to exit the pew. Once they were in the aisle, he took the lead toward the back of the church, where Dale spoke with the last of the congregants.

The older man looked up with a smile as they approached. "Y'all ready to eat? I imagine they're set up by now."

The three of them exited through the front doors and followed the sidewalk around to a separate entrance opening into the fellowship hall. A rush of cold air, noise, and delicious smells met them as they stepped inside.

Long rectangular tables covered with white plastic cloths were staggered around the gymnasium-sized room. Another line of covered tables, these topped with every kind of dish, pot, and plate and loaded with food, stood along the far wall.

A smiling elderly woman with tight gray curls met them at the door. "You're here. Good. Come this way."

She set a brisk pace in her crepe-soled shoes, guiding them to the front of the line where the waiting guests, young and old, gathered. "Pastor Dale, would you ask the blessing, then you all can start things off."

Emily sucked in a breath as one hundred pairs of eyes locked in on the three of them. Oh, no. She cleared her throat to stifle the laughter building in her chest.

"Relax," Noah whispered. "You've got this."

With a move so subtle no one would notice, he closed the distance between them, his upper arm now pressed against her shoulder in a warm, comfortable connection. Immediately, the churning storm inside her ceased.

She blinked. What just happened? There was no physiological explanation as to why a few whispered words and an almost imperceptible touch should calm her when she'd unsuccessfully tried everything to control the inappropriate laugh response.

It didn't make sense. But it worked.

Head bowed as Dale prayed, she snuck a peek at Noah. He winked. Heat shot from her head to her toes and her face flushed as a new, unfamiliar feeling stirred in her chest. Wow.

"Amen."

As soon as Dale finished, the three of them were thrust to the front of the line. Emily picked up a plastic plate and made her way along the laden tables, taking a bit of everything. All those years of medical school and residency, when she'd eaten out of a vending machine or plastic container if she ate at all, had given her a real appreciation for home-cooked food. In no time, her plate was full.

"This way." Dale led them to a table and laid his plate in the center of three places set along the side. Emily took the seat at his left, assuming Noah would take the spot at his right.

She was shocked and flattered when, rather than flanking the pastor, Noah chose to sit on the uncomfortable end so he could be next to her.

"Have you ever seen so many casseroles?" He sounded more horrified than impressed as he lowered onto the metal folding chair, knees splayed to avoid the table legs. "There must be fifty different combinations of chicken and noodles or ground beef and noodles over there."

She'd already had her first bite of one of the chicken options. Delicious. "You're not a fan?"

He lifted his shoulders. "I don't know. I've never had one."

"Never?" She paused, lowering the plastic fork she'd held hovering by her mouth to stare at him. "You've never eaten a casserole? Don't they have covered dishes at your church socials?"

"We don't have church socials." He glanced around the crowded room. "Not like this, anyway. Our church is large. We have about thirty-five thousand attendees at the main campus. Fifteen thousand more at our satellites."

Her brows shot up. Large seemed an inadequate descriptor. "I can see where it'd be tough to seat that many people."

"Our life groups do stuff like this." He picked up his fork and poked suspiciously at the mounds on his plate. "Although they usually meet at restaurants."

Emily hoped no one else noticed the guest of honor playing with his food instead of eating it. He didn't know what he was missing.

She'd just stuffed a forkful of cheesy tomato goodness into her mouth when the Ryders appeared at their table.

"Good morning, Dr. Cutler. We're come to meet Pastor Dale's friend." Mrs. Ryder's coy gaze darted between Noah and Emily. "Obviously you two are already well acquainted."

Hand over her mouth, Emily bobbed her head as she hurriedly chewed a couple more times so she could swallow. Palm up to indicate she hadn't forgotten them, she washed the last bit down with a swig of sweet tea. "Sorry about that. Mr. and Mrs. Ryder, I'd like you to meet Noah Speers. Noah, this is Jane and Mason Ryder."

As smooth as she was awkward, Noah pushed to his feet to greet them warmly. In her defense, it was easier for him because he did not have a mouthful of food.

Over the next hour she watched with a mixture of awe and envy while he dealt with interruption after interruption as the various members of the congregation came by to meet him. Poised and unfailingly polite, he could give lessons to Dale Carnegie on winning friends and influencing people.

Most amazing was his thoughtfulness toward her. At some

point in each conversation, he stopped whomever he spoke with to ask if they had met his friend, Dr. Cutler. He then performed the introductions, allowing her to talk to everyone without bearing the burden of carrying the conversation. For once in her life, she fulfilled her social obligations without embarrassment.

When her mother called later that night for their regular Sunday chat, Emily was still riding the high from her success.

Her mother always began their conversations the same way. "So, how was your day?"

"I met a guy." Oops. The words were out of Emily's mouth before she could stop them. She hadn't intended to mention Noah. The feelings he'd stirred were too new, too wonderful to share.

Her mother hummed with interest. "The four words every mother of a single thirty-year-old wants to hear. Tell me all about him."

Emily closed her eyes to better picture the paragon. A fastidiously dressed food snob who didn't grill or sing, Noah possessed a brilliant smile that stole her breath and a generous spirit that stole her heart.

"He's perfect. And I'm not using the word lightly. He's truly a perfect specimen. Like, he could be featured in a medical textbook. He's tall, six feet or so, wavy blond hair, medium brown eyes, and lean in an athletic sort of way."

Her mother sniffed. "You know I'm not one to be impressed with physical appearance—"

Emily cut her off to stem the disapproving tide. "Normally I'm not either. However, it would be misrepresenting him not to mention that he is gorgeous."

"What about his character?"

"I don't know him well, of course, since we've only just met, but I've had firsthand experience with his kindness."

"Kindness is good." Emily heard the slight thaw in her mother's voice. "What does he do?"

"He's a pastor—technically an executive assistant pastor—for a church in Houston. I don't know much about the church, other than it's one of those large, multicampus churches. He said they have fifty thousand members." And they don't have covered-dish socials.

"Oh. A megachurch." A fresh wave of disapproval came across the phone. "What is someone like that doing in Village Green?"

"Noah is helping out the local pastor until he's feeling better."

Her mother was silent for a moment. "And you say he's interested in you?"

Emily sighed. "Gosh, Mom, do you have to sound so surprised?"

"I'm not surprised that any man would admire you, but from what you've told me . . . let's be honest, he sounds a bit out of your league."

"He's certainly better-looking than I am—"

"*Tsk.* I'm not talking about appearances. I'm talking about experience and expectations. A man like that is a celebrity, like a movie star, and you're . . ."

"Plain."

"Don't put words in my mouth. I was going to say you have a good heart and a good brain." She sighed. "Emily, honey, you're a small-town doctor, not a public figure."

"Yes, but—"

"You have so little experience with men. When was the last time you went on a date?"

"It's been a while."

"It's been years. The last young man you mentioned to me was someone you went out with while you were still in college."

"True, but—"

"I'm just asking you to use caution. This pastor fellow may be a great guy, but with his looks and position he probably travels in a very different circle than you. I would just hate to see you hurt."

After she disconnected the call, Emily remained seated, her legs dangling over the side of her bed. Her mother had a valid point. Emily didn't have a lot of experience with men.

But her mother hadn't seen the wink.

CHAPTER THREE

Noah keyed the address of his first visitation assignment into his phone. Mrs. Dorcas Palmer. Dale said he liked to pop in on Dorcas weekly because of her advanced age. If an eighty-year-old man thought she was old, Mrs. Palmer must be ancient.

Wary of the local police, he kept an eye on the speedometer as he followed the directions through town, if you could call a block or two of mostly empty buildings a town, and out into the country. For a man born and bred in densely populated Houston, this much wide-open space took some getting used to. Those lucky enough to have acreage back home kept it in neatly manicured lawns, like a park. Here the land on either side of the two-lane road spread out in endless undeveloped fields of swaying grasses, golden brown under the August sun, and the occasional stubby tree. He hadn't passed a single car since he'd left downtown.

At the prompt from his GPS, he took a right onto a dirt road marked only by an orange reflector disk on top of a three-foot pole. He traveled the rutted quarter mile to the house at a crawl to prevent ripping out the undercarriage of his car. Each lurch or bounce felt like a personal affront. Who was responsible for filling these potholes? Thick dust enveloped his freshly washed Tesla like a cloud. Sheesh. Why hadn't someone paved this miserable excuse for a road?

He pulled up in front of a small white clapboard house that

made Dale's place look grand and cut off the engine. *Okay, Lord. Here goes nothing.*

He scooped his Bible off the passenger seat and climbed out of the car. Unsure of the accepted protocol for a pastoral visit and too embarrassed to expose his ignorance to Dale by asking for instructions, he'd brought it along because it seemed like a pastoral thing to do. And if they ran out of things to talk about, which seemed likely, he could always offer to read.

Dorcas was old. If her eyesight was bad, maybe she'd like that. He'd mentally prepared the Twenty-third Psalm. Short and sweet.

While crossing the hard-packed dirt toward the house, he noted that the boards on several of the stairs leading up to the porch were rotted. It was a toss-up whether the deteriorated top step would support his weight. He frowned. This place, starting with the road leading to it, was a health hazard. Somebody needed to fix this.

Cautiously he climbed the stairs, sidestepping the worst places, and crossed to the entrance. Seeing no doorbell, he tucked the Bible under his left arm and knocked. If she was as old as he feared, thinking Methuselah now, she was probably deaf. He knocked again, harder.

The door swung open and a wrinkled, fragile-looking woman with an angelic halo of pure white curls stood on the other side. She was dressed in a faded floral garment that snapped up the front— a dress or maybe a robe—and a pair of pink terry-cloth slippers. Tenting a blue-veined hand over her eyes, she squinted up at him. "Where's the fire?"

He glanced behind him. "I'm sorry?"

She jabbed a sharp finger into his chest. "I asked where the fire was, young man. Certainly, that's the only reason you'd beat on my door until I feared it would fall in."

Not fragile then. "No, ma'am. No fire. Sorry if I frightened you. I just didn't know if you could hear my knock."

"My ears are fine. It's my knees that are crap."

Nor angelic. She must have noted the way his jaw dropped. "Don't give me that look. A woman my age has earned the right to say whatever she wants, Preacher Man."

"I wasn't aware there was an age limit on polite speech." He clamped his lips together. He needed to build rapport, not scold her. He'd never get this meeting over with if he didn't get in the door. He sent her a smile. "But if that's as bad as it gets, I believe I can let you off with a warning. How'd you know I'm a preacher?"

She pointed a gnarled hand toward him. "Those fancy duds and that big ol' Bible were my first clue. Besides, Dale called to tell me you were coming."

Noah ignored the uncharitable thought that Dale could have visited with her on the phone and saved him the trip. "Dale said he likes to come out every week to see you, and since he's having back trouble, he asked if I'd stop by in his place."

"Poor Dale's always having trouble with his da—er . . ." She stopped and sent him a sassy yellowed smile that was missing a few teeth. "Darn back."

Noah laughed in spite of himself. He liked the crusty old girl. "Good save." He extended a hand to her. "Let's make it official. I'm Noah Speers."

She placed her hand in his, her bones delicate in his grasp. "Noah's a good Bible name. I like it."

Now they were getting somewhere. "Thank you. Dorcas is also a good Bible name."

Frowning, she snatched her hand away. "Dorcas is lame. I can't imagine what my mother was thinking to saddle me with a name like that. I took crap from kids about it my whole life." She gave him a wary look through rheumy eyes. "Oops. I said crap again, didn't I? It just slipped out."

He didn't laugh since it would only encourage her. "It happens. What name would you prefer?"

"Esther." Her quick response said she'd given the matter some thought. "Now *that's* a good Bible name."

He nodded. "Fit for a queen."

"Exactly."

"Tell you what. If you'd like, I'd be happy to call you Esther. It can be your nickname."

She cocked her head from side to side as she considered his offer, her movements reminding him of a bird. "That'd be fine." She turned. "Come on in and we'll sit for a while."

"Thank you." He followed her into the shadowy, musty-smelling house. "I should warn you, I've never done a church visitation before. You'll have to show me the ropes."

She stopped suddenly, rearing back as if *he'd* cussed, and glared at him through narrowed eyes. "What kind of pastor doesn't check on his people?"

He raised his hands shoulder high in surrender. "I'm a specialized pastor. Right now, I handle the administrative side of the church."

"Never heard of a specialized pastor. *Tsk.* That's no excuse for neglecting your people." She led him to a small sitting room and pointed him to a faded green armchair. "Have a seat. I guess the fact you're here to see me counts for something. I'll show you how to go about a proper visit, then you can get to doing the Lord's work."

He doubted Queen Esther herself was more adept at issuing orders. "Thank you."

The room was small and square, with a good-sized window along one wall. The open curtains flooded the space with natural light.

Dorcas apparently didn't subscribe to minimalism in her decorating. She'd crammed the maximum amount of furniture into the room—another chair, a loveseat, two end tables, a coffee table, and an upright piano. Every available surface was topped with knick-knacks and books.

She seated herself at the piano, swinging her legs around the side of the bench so she faced the instrument, her back to him. "First thing we'll do is sing a couple of hymns. I wasn't in church this Sunday because my da—er, durn knees were giving me fits, so I missed the singing. It's my favorite part."

Oh no. "Why don't you sing, and I'll be your audience?"

With a huff, she swiveled around to face him, bony arms folded across her chest. "Who is teaching who? If you're going to get this visiting business right, then you're going to have to sing."

She handed him a hymnal. "Go ahead and pick out your favorite."

"Dorcas—I mean, Esther—I'm not a singer." His tone carried a plea.

"If you're worried about the words, don't. I've got my own hymnal right here." She pointed to the top of her piano.

"It's not the words. I'm a terrible singer." There, he'd admitted it.

"Me, too." She dismissed his confession with an easy wave. "The Lord tells us to make a joyful noise, so that's what we'll do."

Clearly, she wouldn't be satisfied until she thoroughly humiliated him, so he flipped through the hymnal, looking for a short, easy song. "How about 'Amazing Grace'?"

As soon as the words were out of his mouth, she started to play from memory, her gnarled fingers expertly handling the worn keys. She gave him a two-measure intro, at the correct tempo, then a brisk nod signaling him to begin.

Dorcas, aka Esther, was an enthusiastic singer. A terrible, enthusiastic singer. She warbled off-key at the top of her lungs which, while painful to listen to, suited him just fine. All he had to do was mouth the words, letting her drown him out.

Halfway through the first verse she stopped, turned to him, and narrowed her eyes. "I can't hear you."

"I'm singing." *Sort of.* He lifted the hymnal as proof.

The frown she sent him said she wasn't buying it. "Not loud enough. The whole purpose of singing together is for everyone to participate. It's more fun that way."

No. No part of this classified as fun. "Yes, ma'am."

She swiveled back around to face the keys. "I'll start again. At the beginning." And no doubt would continue to restart until he cooperated.

This time when she gave him the intro and a signal to start, he didn't hold back. He gave his all—the full bullfrog. Instead of recoiling in horror, she smiled, bobbing her head as she added her caterwauling to his croaking. Hard to say who sang worse, but the combination sounded like a barnyard massacre.

As the notes of the second hymn, "What a Friend We Have in Jesus," faded, Noah reached for his Bible and hurriedly flipped it open to prevent a painful third. "Wow, look at the time. I need to be on my way. Why don't I read a psalm before I leave? Do you have a favorite?"

He already had a finger marking the twenty-third when she turned and angled a canny gaze at him. "I particularly like the One-hundred-nineteenth Psalm."

Of course. He bit back a sigh. The longest psalm.

"The whole thing." Her eyes held a challenge. "I want to hear it all."

"Yes, ma'am."

"And not too fast." Her expression was sly. "I'm a slow listener."

He read every bit of it. All 176 verses. Slowly. Several times he'd glanced her way and noticed she mouthed the psalm along with him. The old rascal had it memorized.

"You have a nice way of reading Scripture, Preacher Man. You may come back and visit me next week, and we'll do this again." The implication being he could use the practice.

He stood. "Thank you for your kind invitation, but I won't be here next week." *Please, God.* "Dale is on the mend, and I need to head back to my church in Houston."

For a moment her wrinkled face fell, and he felt a twinge of remorse. Poor old girl must not get much company out here. Then her cloudy eyes lit. "No worries. You can come later this week. I'm not busy on Friday. Plan to stay for lunch, and I'll make you one of my tuna sandwiches."

Outmaneuvered, with no way of escape, Noah struggled to keep the smile on his face. "Sounds delicious, Dorcas." It took a second to figure out why she gave him the stink eye. "I mean, Esther."

She grinned. "Run along, Preacher Man. See you Friday."

Emily had seen five patients by lunch, an increase over the previous week, which had been an increase over the week before that. When she'd accepted the challenge of establishing a practice in an underserved area, they'd warned her startup would be slow. It took time to get the word out, and longer still for the locals to decide to transfer their health care to her. Before she'd opened, the closest medical clinic was thirty minutes away in Corsicana, and most of Village Green traveled there for treatment.

The chamber of commerce, who'd been instrumental in bringing her to town, had sent out a community-wide mailing announcing the opening of the clinic. In addition, she'd introduced herself as the new doctor to most of Dale's small congregation, who probably constituted half the population. As far as she could tell, the word was out. Still, it would take time to gain a foothold.

There were upsides to the small caseload. She loved that she could spend quality time with each patient, getting to know more about them than their vitals and a list of symptoms. One of the reasons she'd chosen family medicine was the potential to build relationships with her patients as well as treat them.

The abundant downtime in week one allowed her to get to know the support team the university had hired for her—a thirty-year-old medical assistant named Jodi, and Candy, her fifty-something office manager/receptionist—and to set up the clinic the way they wanted it. The one-story brick building, a block from downtown, had been boarded up for twenty years since the last doctor had retired. When her alma mater, TBU, decided to plant a clinic in Village Green, they'd acquired the space, updated the plumbing and HVAC systems, replaced the flooring, and painted the interior.

Monday and Tuesday, before opening their doors to the public while the work crews finished out the building, Emily and her team prepped the office for business. With her twenty-five years of experience in medical offices, Candy had no trouble setting up the programs and protocols they needed, while Jodi and Emily unpacked and put away the supplies in the exam rooms and storage closet.

Emily brought in lunch both days, partially to limit the interruption to their work, and mostly so they could build bonds. The three women shared food, stories, and laughter around a folding table Emily set up in the waiting room. At the conclusion of day two, they also shared the conviction that, while the university had done a top-notch job upgrading the old building, things looked too institutional. Functional, but not attractive. Since they had no budget for decorating, each woman agreed to go home to scavenge potential decorations. By Wednesday, with the addition of the plants and wall décor they'd contributed, sourced either from home or from craft and hobby shops, they'd transformed the utilitarian space into a cheerful medical office.

During week two, Emily spent her non-patient time setting up her office. She carefully unwrapped her massive framed medical school diploma from its protective box. While humming a rousing rendition of "Pomp and Circumstance," she hung it on the wall behind the beat-up desk they'd salvaged from the previous tenant's furniture. After admiring the diploma for an indecently long time, she added the few textbooks she'd saved from medical school to an equally beat-up bookcase on the opposite wall.

When she could set aside some money, she planned to buy a rug and a lamp or two to add some color and light to the windowless room. Even now, with its dinged furniture and nearly bare walls, the small space delighted her. All those years of work and sacrifice paid off. Dr. Emily Cutler finally hung out her shingle.

By the end of the second week, the surfeit of free time wore on her nerves. Active by nature and conditioned by four years of medical school and another three years of residency to operate at full speed, she didn't know what to do with the inactivity.

She read up on the conditions she'd seen in her new patients, checked online sites for important medical news and updates, and played word games on her phone. For the first time ever, she was bored.

Then Noah walked into her life.

Tall and blond, and too beautiful for words, thoughts of him filled the restless gaps in her time. After their initial Saturday night meeting over burgers at Dale's, her ruminations centered on her awkwardness and total unsuitability for such a perfect specimen.

The whole laughing thing? She shuddered at the memory. Not her finest hour.

Even yesterday morning when she showed up at his pew, everything about his body language confirmed her unwanted status. Men like him weren't interested in women like her.

Then suddenly, inexplicably, and certainly miraculously, everything changed. She admitted to him she was an introvert, and somehow her confessed vulnerability and acute discomfort in crowds opened the door for communication and relationship between them. Like any good hero, Noah rose to the challenge of protecting her, and in doing so, his eyes were opened to her previously unappreciated inner beauty.

The sensible side of her argued she was reading too much into a simple act of kindness. However unromantic, it was definitely a possibility.

Just when she'd semi-convinced her more dominant, rational self that he was simply a nice guy doing a good deed, she'd remember the wink, and rational thought flew out the window. Who knew the rapid closing and opening of a single eyelid could produce such sensations? If she focused on the memory, she could still feel the flash of heat followed immediately by palpitations. A wink that powerful surely conveyed deep emotion.

And when he leaned into her, pressing his arm to her shoulder? Didn't that say he liked her? That he wanted a deeper connection?

Since last night, Emily's thoughts had seesawed between the absolute assurance of a burgeoning romance to the complete conviction that she was an idiot to imagine she could capture the attention and heart of such a man. So, this morning, when she walked her last patient to the door and saw the empty waiting room, she wasn't disappointed as she'd been in the past, but delighted she had time to disappear into her office and indulge in a bit of pleasant daydreaming over her peanut butter and jelly sandwich.

She'd run through all the reasons why he'd never be interested in her and had eaten half her sandwich when there was a knock at her door.

"Dr. Cutler?" Jodi popped her head in, eyes wide with excitement. "There's a Noah Speers in the front, asking to speak to you."

The unexpected announcement caused Emily to inhale sharply and choke on the last little bit of sandwich in her mouth.

"Would you bring him to my office please?" she managed between hacking coughs.

Heart hammering against her ribs, she rewrapped the remainder of the sandwich and hid it in the top drawer of her desk. Noah wanted to talk to her?

The combination of shock mixed with equal doses of joy and trepidation muddled her usually clear thinking. Why did he want to speak to her?

Should she greet him at the door or welcome him from behind her desk? Wobbly knees would be less noticeable from behind the desk. Should she sit or stand? She didn't want to block her diploma, did she? She settled on sitting behind her desk, hands folded on her blotter. Professional yet approachable.

Another knock and the object of her dreams strode into her office. If possible, he was better looking than she remembered. Tall and confident, he wore a blue dress shirt, unbuttoned at the neck, and a pair of tailored khaki slacks. Even in the wilting August heat, he managed to look fresh and crisp. His golden hair lay molded to his head, not one strand out of place.

He flashed a brilliant white smile. "Hi, Emily. Thanks for seeing me."

"Absolutely." She gestured toward the armchairs in front of her desk. "Please, have a seat."

Halfway across the room he stopped, eyes on her, his beautiful face creased in concern. "Are you okay?"

Her hands stole up to her cheeks. "Yes. Why?"

He continued to study her. "Your face is splotchy and red, and your eyes look watery, like you've been crying."

"Oh, ha ha." Her laugh sounded forced. "No, some of my sandwich got caught in my throat." She patted the front of her neck. "I'm fine now."

He pushed up his sleeve to glance at his expensive-looking watch. "It's straight-up noon." He frowned. "I'm sorry. I didn't even think about the time. Am I interrupting your lunch?"

There it was again. His trademark thoughtfulness. And what did it mean that he'd forgotten the time? Could it be that his thoughts were as tangled up in her as hers were in him?

"Not at all," she lied. "I'm glad you stopped by. Please, sit."

He sat in the scarred chair directly across from her and surveyed the room. "So, this is your office."

Her gaze followed the same path his had taken. In light of his sophistication and polished perfection, the room suddenly seemed dark and cramped and maybe even a little seedy. "It needs some work," she admitted. "I inherited the furniture from the previous doctor."

He rubbed his hands along the worn arms of the chair. "It seems . . . sturdy."

She nodded. "And when I've saved a little money, I plan to add some lamps and a rug, to make the room more cozy."

"I'm sure you'll fix it up really nice." He leaned forward, resting his forearms on his thighs, and sent her a million-dollar smile. "I won't keep you, since I imagine you've got patients coming in, but I've been thinking about us and yesterday."

Oh. My. Gosh. She hadn't been crazy. He *was* attracted to her. Wait till she told her mom. Heat warmed her cheeks as she held his gaze. "Me too."

"I figured you would. It was so obvious. First dinner on

Saturday, then the pew and table arrangements on Sunday—bless Dale's heart."

Her smile faded and brows knit as she tried to figure out what Dale had to do with this. Aha! He introduced them. Yes, bless Dale's heart for his interference.

"This morning at breakfast I asked him if he was playing match-maker, and he admitted he was."

And bless Dale's heart for seeing the possibilities and bringing them together.

"I asked him to knock it off."

Made sense. Bless Dale's heart for getting the ball rolling. Of course, now that they'd found each other, they could let true love take its course.

"I know his intentions were good, he's such a nice guy, but that was really embarrassing for both of us." Noah leaned back in the chair and laughed. "Can you think of any two people who are less suited to each other than you and me?"

Less suited? Emily froze. At his invitation to join in on the joke, she tried to laugh, but it sounded more like a sob caught in her throat. Less suited? He'd come here to tell her he wasn't interested?

"Anyway, I knew you'd noticed the whole matchmaking thing too, so I thought I'd let you know I've asked him to stop." He smiled. "You're safe now. He won't be throwing us together anymore."

She forced a half smile onto her frozen face. "I appreciate you letting me know."

"No problem." He pushed to his feet. "I'll let you get back to work. Have a great afternoon, Doc."

And in his thoughtful way, with a warm smile and a nod of his perfect head, Beauty broke the heart of the Beast.

Dale wasn't surprised to see his friend Jim's number appear on his phone screen. "I figured you'd be checking up on us."

"You know me too well." Jim laughed. "So, what do you think of our boy?"

"Noah's impressive. Handsome, intelligent, self-possessed. He looks like what I imagine a young CEO of a Fortune Five Hundred company looks like."

"But not much like a pastor."

"I didn't say that."

"You didn't have to." Jim sighed. "My grandson is a great guy, my pride and joy, but he's far from perfect. His parents and I have spoiled him rotten. I'm not proud of that. We've done him a disservice, one that I'm determined to correct before he steps into a more public role at the church. I don't know a more gifted, humble servant of God than you, Dale. I want him to watch you at work. Hopefully some of your example will rub off on him."

"Thank you for the compliment and confidence. You know I'm happy to help, but I won't be able to keep him here long. My back wasn't too bad to start with, and by now it's pretty much good as new."

"No! You can't send him home yet. You have to stay infirm a bit longer."

Dale paused. "I hate to be dishonest."

"*Pah*, it's for the sake of the kingdom. Remember when King David pretended to be insane?"

"I do. I also remember the half-dozen harebrained schemes you put us up to while we were in seminary. I'm trying to decide which circumstance more mirrors this current scheme of yours."

"Good times, my friend." Jim laughed. "Don't pull the plug on this yet. Noah's got the leadership and speaking parts down cold. It's the servanthood we need to work on."

CHAPTER FOUR

Noah's stomach rumbled as he emerged from his bedroom a little after eight Tuesday morning. His quiet time had been so fruitful, it'd been tough breaking away.

When he'd awakened the previous Sunday, the first thing he'd noticed was the profound silence, like a thick blanket of snow, that settled over the remote little house in the early hours. Ironically, to a man accustomed to the buzz of the city, the hum of traffic, and the whirrs and dings of technology, the quiet was distracting. He couldn't concentrate.

Yet, as he had pressed into Scripture and prayer that morning, and each morning since, the hush became a holy silence—a space where he could lean into God and discern His voice.

Had he stumbled upon the one upside to living at the edge of the world?

His smile fell as he stepped into the hall and noted the door to Dale's room was closed. Unusual. The old guy habitually got up with the dawn and had coffee and breakfast ready when Noah got to the table.

He proceeded to the kitchen and flipped on the overhead light. No sign of breakfast prep. No delicious smells. The coffee pot sat cold and empty.

He glanced back toward Dale's room with an uneasy frown. Was he okay? Honestly, with old people you could never be sure.

After some internal debate, Noah tapped lightly on Dale's door and, at his invitation, swung it open. The older man sat in bed, dressed in his pajamas, propped up on a mound of white pillows.

Noah took a tentative step into the room. "Are you okay?"

Dale lowered the book he was reading and removed his glasses. He smiled. "I'm fine. I've decided to give my back some extra rest."

Uh oh. That couldn't be good. "Can I get something for you?"

Dale nodded. "Coffee and something to eat would be nice. I'm sorry I didn't get up to prepare anything. I felt it . . . wisest to remain in bed."

"I understand. I'll be happy to make us some coffee and breakfast. Give me a little bit, and I'll bring it to you."

"Thank you, Noah." The older man waved him off. "You're a good man."

Noah withdrew into the hall and smacked his forehead with the heel of his hand. What was he thinking? Why would he offer to make breakfast when he didn't have a clue about cooking?

First things first. He needed coffee. Dale's machine dated back to the dark ages, before some genius invented those handy little pods that, when dropped into a high-tech device, produced an excellent cup of coffee. He knew from yesterday's drive through town that Village Green didn't offer a Starbucks or coffee shop where he could access caffeine and breakfast through the window of his car.

His gaze fell on the antiquated coffee maker, and he took a deep breath. It was up to him and the relic. He pulled his phone from his pocket and googled the process for brewing coffee in this particular model.

The kitchen was small and the cabinets few, so it didn't take long to locate the cups, measuring spoons, and filters. The can of coffee sat on the top shelf of the refrigerator.

As per the instructions, he filled the water to the proper line, fitted the filter into the machine, measured the appropriate amount of coffee, and pressed the On button. In seconds the sounds and smells emanating from the appliance indicated he had successfully brewed his first pot of coffee. *Woohoo.*

Heady with success, Noah reopened the refrigerator, looking for their main course. The carton of eggs and package of bacon seemed too challenging for his first attempt at breakfast. Maybe it would be wiser to ease into the whole domestic thing.

Ten minutes after their first conversation, Noah reappeared at Dale's door. "Knock, knock. Breakfast is served." He entered bearing a bowl of cereal and a cup of black coffee on a cookie sheet he'd repurposed as a tray.

"Thank you so much. Why don't you put it on the table here?" Dale pointed to the nightstand beside his bed. "It looks wonderful."

"Now I know you're just being nice." Noah transferred the Cheerios and coffee mug to the table and straightened, tucking the cookie sheet under his arm. "As a novice, I admit I'm pretty proud of how everything turned out, but you'd have to be extremely hungry to think a bowl of cereal looks wonderful."

Dale set his book aside and reached for the coffee. "Novice? You don't cook?"

"No, sir."

The older man sipped before regarding Noah over the rim of the mug. "Not interested?"

Noah shrugged. "Never learned how. Cooking for one seems like a lot of work, especially when I have access to everything I want through takeout and delivery. What about you? Do you like to cook?"

"I don't mind it." Dale replaced the coffee on the nightstand and picked up the bowl of cereal and spoon. "I learned after I lost my Betty. I'll never be the cook she was, but I won't starve."

Each time Dale spoke about his wife, Noah glimpsed an undercurrent of sorrow. She'd been gone for ten years and yet he still mourned her. It saddened him to know the gentle man was hurting. "Everything I've eaten here has been good."

Dale smiled. "Thank you. If you're interested in learning, I'd be happy to teach you what I know."

Honestly, he couldn't imagine what he'd do with the knowledge, but why not? It wasn't like he had anything better to do.

"Yeah. Okay. I'd like that." Noah glanced around the tidy room. "Can I get you anything before I go?"

Dale pointed to the cereal with his spoon. "This is fine."

Noah moved to the door. "After I finish my coffee, I'll get cleaned up and head out to make my visits. Will you be okay while I'm gone?"

The older man smiled. "Sure. I'll start working on my sermon for next week. Probably won't surface until dinner."

Halfway into the hall, a thought occurred to Noah. He stopped, turned around, and popped his head back in the door. "Don't start dinner until I get here. If you tell me what to do, I can handle it."

Dale grinned. "It's a deal."

Noah pulled up in front of the red brick clinic a little before noon. The printed sign hanging from a cord inside the glass front door said Open, so he parked and walked in.

The middle-aged lady at the front desk looked up from her

computer and smiled in recognition. "Hello, Pastor Speers. What can I do for you today?"

"Hi. Is Dr. Cutler available?"

She sent him a quizzical look. "Is this regarding a medical issue? Do you need an appointment?"

He grinned. "No. I just thought she might like to take a break and grab some lunch."

"I don't know what her plans are." She smiled and picked up the phone. "Let me call back there and tell her you're here."

"Thank you."

The waiting room stood empty. He'd been cooped up all morning, so rather than sit on one of the gray plastic chairs lined up along the walls, he walked around. Someone went to a lot of trouble to make the place cheerful, with pots of plants at the windows and colorful prints on the walls. The magazines on the tables were even current.

The door in the back of the room opened and Emily stepped out, a white lab coat over her clothes and a puzzled frown on her face.

He took a step toward her, stopping when he saw her expression. "Uh oh. Did I come at a bad time?"

"No." She continued to frown as she studied him. "I'm just surprised to see you."

"Sorry. I should have called ahead." He tried to inject some enthusiasm into the awkward moment. "I thought we could go grab some lunch."

Her dark brows furrowed. "We? You and me? Now?"

He gave her a shrug and amped up his smile. "What better time than lunch time?"

"No, I don't think so. I brought my lunch—"

He jumped in before she could turn him down. "Save it for dinner. Come on, Doc. Help me out here. I'm desperate."

A wince passed across her face.

"No. Sorry. That didn't come out right. What I meant to say is I'm desperate to talk to someone my own age. Or decade. I've spent the morning with wrinkles; I'm going to spend the afternoon with wrinkles." He sighed heavily. "You get the picture."

That made her smile. "Church visitations?"

He bobbed his head. "A slew of them. My capacity for small talk has been stretched to the limit." He sent her a pleading glance. "Lunch with a friend would go a long way in fortifying me for the afternoon."

He liked the way her blue eyes sparkled when she laughed. "Okay, I'll go. But I can only be gone for an hour. I've got patients coming in this afternoon."

If Emily had made a list of one hundred possible outcomes for today, having lunch with Noah would not be on it. After yesterday's crushing conversation, she expected to catch a glimpse of him at church or not at all.

Last night she'd gone home and had a good cry over the death of her foolish imaginings, then put them aside. People like her didn't end up with men like him. Lesson learned.

So, to have him show up at the clinic and ask her to lunch was shocking. It stung a bit, like pulling a bandage off tender flesh, to hear him say he was there out of desperation, but the reminder of their unsuitability helped cement the lesson in her mind.

And, being new to town, she understood what it was like to be lonely and need a friend.

She glanced over her shoulder toward the interior door she'd just come through. "Give me a second, and I'll grab my purse."

He smiled. "Lunch is on me since you're doing me a massive favor. I don't know what's available, so you'll have to tell me where you want to eat."

"Ha ha! You're kidding, right? You know there's only one restaurant in Village Green." The horrified look he sent her said he didn't know. "But don't worry. The food there is delicious."

After she hung up her lab coat and gathered her bag from her office, she rejoined him in the waiting room, and they stepped outside into the bright sunlight together. The weatherman had predicted one hundred degrees today. Apparently, he'd underestimated.

"How far is it?" Noah slipped on a pair of mirrored sunglasses that made him look like a movie star. "Do we walk?"

She pointed to his car. "Ordinarily I'd say yes, it's good exercise, but since I've never ridden in a Tesla and probably will never have the opportunity again, I would prefer it if you drove."

The masculine assurance in his smile was enough to raise the already scorching temperature outdoors another two degrees. He opened the passenger door, and she slid onto the cushiony seat.

"Wow." She ran an appreciative hand over the ivory leather even as the practical side of her cringed. Seriously, who drove a car with white upholstery?

He climbed in on the driver's side and started the engine. He glanced over to get her reaction. "Do you like it?"

"It's amazing." With a glass roof and nothing on the dash except a computer touch screen, it looked more like a spaceship than a car. "It's probably worth more than my parents' home."

"It'll go zero to sixty in two-point-three seconds."

She resisted the temptation to roll her eyes. What was it about guys and the speed of their cars? His comment, so much like something one of her younger brothers would say, helped put things in perspective. While Noah Speers epitomized perfection, he was also very human. She could be herself around him.

"Not in Village Green, it won't, or you'll be facing a big fat fine."

He grinned. "Good point. So where are we headed?"

"One block over." She pointed toward the west. "Estelle's. There's parking on Main Street."

From the corner of her eye, she watched as he drove the short distance to the restaurant. Man and machine were a perfect complement to each other. Both were sleek and elegant, high-powered, and a bit impractical.

And entirely out of her league.

He pulled into one of the diagonal parking spots outside the restaurant and shut off the car, leaning forward for a better look through the windshield. After a quick study, he turned to her with a worried frown. "This is it?"

She sent him a wide smile. "Trust me. It's delicious."

The owner met them at the cash register just inside the door. Country music, conversation, and delicious smells filled the air. "Hi, Dr. Cutler. Good to see you."

"Hello, Estelle. Noah and I are here for lunch."

Noting the older woman's stupefied stare, she added, "I see you haven't met. This is Pastor Noah Speers. He's visiting Dale."

Speechless, Estelle bobbed her head. Emily understood. She'd had a similar reaction to all that beauty.

"We'll just find a seat." Emily pointed. "I think I see one by the window."

Noah followed her through the crowd to an empty table and took the chair across from her. He glanced around the room. "They do a big business."

"I'm sure it helps they're the only game in town, but the food is really good." Emily took two laminated menus from behind the chrome napkin dispenser and handed one to him. "The specials are on the front. Tuesday is chicken-fried steak. It's delicious."

Brows lifted, his eyes met hers. "What kind of doctor recommends fried food?"

She grinned. "A hungry one. I certainly wouldn't endorse a diet high in fried foods, but you appear to be in good health, and I'm a firm believer that the occasional splurge is therapeutic."

"If you say so." He scanned one side of the menu then flipped to the back. "Where are the salads?"

She laughed out loud. "Don't look now but your big city roots are showing. This is rural Texas, Noah. You won't find many salad entrees around here."

He grinned. "You're right." He dropped the menu behind the napkin holder. "Fried food it is. When in Podunk, do as the Podunkians do."

When Estelle arrived at the table to take their order, they both asked for the special—his with the gravy on the side—and mashed potatoes and green beans. Sweet tea to drink.

Noah waited for the older woman to leave before leaning in toward Emily and lowering his voice. "So how long before you can bust out of here?"

No misunderstanding his question. He'd made his opinion of the small town crystal clear. "I'll have fulfilled my contract in four years."

"And then what?" Noah's knee bounced beneath the table. Energy rolled off him in palpable waves. "You strike me as a woman with goals—you wouldn't have become a doctor without them. What does the future hold for Dr. Cutler?"

"I'm not sure. For the first time in my life, my future is not scripted. I've known since I was a kid that I wanted to be a doctor, so every step I've taken up to this point was carefully planned. The classes I took, the schools I attended, even the way I spent my summers were orchestrated to get me where I am today. Now that I'm here, I have the luxury to wait and listen for what the Lord has next."

"I wouldn't think a wait-and-listen posture would be comfortable for a woman with ambition. In my experience, if you want big results, you've got to make big plans and go for it."

She folded her arms on the table and looked him squarely in the eyes. "Who says I want big results?"

He sputtered. The most attractive, polished, and self-confident man she'd even known tripped over his silver tongue while he searched for the words to express his obvious frustration and disapproval of her answer.

"Of course, you do." He finally found his voice, slightly raised now with the passion of his convictions. "You've dedicated seven extra years of your life beyond college to be trained as a physician. Surely you want to use your talents and education and sacrifice for the greatest good. It would be criminal for you to fritter them away."

The argument was not a new one. She'd heard it from friends and colleagues the moment she'd made her decision. They questioned her sanity in choosing to bury herself in the anonymity of a small town rather than pursue the advancement and prestige available in bigger areas.

"I'm not convinced the greatest good always equals big results."

More sputtering. This time he added a reddened face.

She lifted a hand to silence the argument she saw brewing. He couldn't say anything she hadn't already heard.

Because it mattered to her that he understand, she tried to explain. "You're correct. I am ambitious, even a bit driven. But I think I measure success differently than you. I like making money, obviously I have bills to pay, and I enjoy recognition as much as the next person, but those things aren't enough. Life isn't a race to do more. Our purpose on earth is to become more like Christ."

She hadn't meant to sound preachy. "God knows me better than anyone. He knows my need to contribute, to feel significant, to serve in a meaningful way. So, when I asked Him to lead me to the right position, I believe He did."

Eyes locked with hers, he sat in silence, tapping his long fingers on the table. His penetrating gaze lingered on her face, studying her while he weighed her words. At last he spoke, his brows lifted in question. "And if He says He wants you to stay in Village Green?"

Emily smiled. "Then I'll do it with pleasure, knowing I'm right in the center of His will."

He broke eye contact to glance out the window. "I'm pretty doubtful anything about this place figures into His will."

She laughed at his stubborn determination to see only the warts of her newly adopted home. "Come on. It's not *that* bad. Be serious. Other than a rough start, what have you got against Village Green?"

Pushing up his sleeve, he made a show of glancing at the gleaming watch on his wrist before looking at her. "I don't think we've got enough time, if I have to get you back in an hour."

No way she'd let him off that easily. "Give me the highlights."

He cocked a thumb. "It's small. Like even at an insulting thirty miles an hour, you can make it through the entire town in two minutes."

She nodded. Can't argue with facts.

"There's nothing to do here. No theaters, museums, or malls." He continued to tick his grievances off on his long, elegant fingers. "No coffee shops or dry cleaners. One restaurant in the whole town."

She felt compelled to offer some defense of her home. "There's a fantastic bakery next door."

He threw up his hands in mock surrender. "There you go. And here I thought we were in the boonies."

"You wouldn't be so snarky if you'd tasted her blueberry scones."

His eyes lit with humor. "Fine. It has a decent bakery. That doesn't make up for the shortage of everything else." He lowered his voice to a whisper. "Or the fact the entire population is ancient."

"It does have a high percentage of seniors."

"Seniors?" Noah was back to full volume. And then some. "You're a very generous woman, Dr. Cutler. Most of the people I've met in the last three days make Methuselah look like a youngster. Yesterday, I spent the morning with a woman who appears to be a hundred years old. And swears."

Grinning, Emily nodded. "Dorcas Palmer."

"You've met her?"

She laughed at the combined horror and surprise on his face. "Yes. For the record she's ninety-seven. And quite a pistol."

"*Quite a pistol* must be small-town speak for a terror. Whatever. I was legitimately traumatized by my visit to the old girl, and to make matters worse, she conned me into a second one on Friday. She wants to fix me lunch."

The laughter died in Emily's throat. "Oh, no. Not the tuna."

He stilled. "What?"

She paused, giving herself a moment to choose her words. "Maybe I just had a bad experience, but the tuna she served me bore an unhappy resemblance to cat food."

Noah blanched.

Grimacing at the memory, she nodded. "My suggestion? You bring lunch to her. She told me she loves fried chicken."

Brows furrowed, he appeared to give the suggestion serious thought. "I don't know if I can learn to fry chicken by Friday."

Her eyes shot wide. "You're learning to cook?" She'd have been much less surprised if he'd said he was learning to hang glide.

The way he dropped his gaze was endearingly self-conscious. "Another story for another time."

Except there wouldn't be another time. Her wonderful, funny new friend would soon be returning to his sophisticated life. She pushed the thought away. No point in lamenting what she couldn't have. Instead, she'd be grateful for the short acquaintance.

"Estelle's makes delicious fried chicken. Stop by here on your way out to Dorcas's and pick up lunch. She'll be delighted, you'll be a hero, and I won't get a call in the middle of the night asking for something to counteract severe gastric distress."

"Good idea. Thanks." Heartfelt gratitude shone all over his handsome face. "You may have saved my life."

She met his smile with an answering grin. "You may be right. And you're welcome."

Estelle arrived and slid a loaded plate in front of each of them. After placing their glasses of tea on the table and asking if they had everything they needed, she took one last, forgivably long look at Noah and left.

He eyed his plate with interest. "It smells good." He sounded surprised.

"Yes, it does, doubting Thomas." She placed her napkin in her lap. "Just wait till you taste it. Would you ask the blessing, and we can start?"

They bowed their heads while he said a quick prayer. Emily believed you could tell a lot about a person by the way they prayed in public. Noah's prayer was softly spoken, no showy grab for attention from nearby patrons, and delivered as conversationally as though he was conversing with a dear friend. Nice.

"Amen." Noah picked up his knife and fork. She watched with interest as he cut off the corner of his steak, dipped it tentatively into the bowl of cream gravy, and put it in his mouth.

"So?" For all her brave talk, she was actually apprehensive about his reaction.

Busy chewing and clearly too polite to speak with his mouth

full, he nodded vigorously. Once he swallowed, he put down his utensils and smiled. "Okay. I admit it; you were right. It's amazing. Really. One of the best things I've put in my mouth."

"Told you." She sliced off a bit of her steak. "It may be the only restaurant in town, but it's a good one."

They didn't speak for a minute or two while each focused on the meal. Though small in stature, Emily could put away a lot of food, earning her the moniker of *lumberjack* in medical school.

"How's Dale today?"

Noah looked up from his lunch and frowned. "Not as well as I expected. He was still in bed when I got up. Ordinarily he'd have been up for hours and have breakfast ready."

Emily stilled. "Did he say he was in pain?"

He shook his head. "No. And he didn't have that pinched look people get when they're suffering. He said he was being cautious."

"Makes sense." Though it didn't sound like the Dale she knew. "I'll call him this afternoon and see how he is."

"Good idea." Noah sighed. "When I agreed to come to Village Green, it was supposed to be a quick trip. Three days tops. Then I agreed to take on Dale's visitation schedule. Even after extending my stay a couple of days, I figured I could still get out of here by late Friday. If he has a setback . . ." Another sigh. His brown eyes said all the words his lips refused to speak.

She nodded sympathetically. "I'm sorry. I know you're eager to get back to Houston."

At the mention of home, his million-dollar smile returned. "You have no idea. Even after enjoying an outstanding meal with excellent company, I can state unequivocally that Village Green is *not* in God's will for me."

CHAPTER FIVE

"K nives or fingers?"

Noah looked over at his apron-wearing host standing beside him in the tiny kitchen. "Tough call. Since I have no idea what you're talking about, I'm going to require more information before I can give you my decision."

Dale grinned and nodded. "Ah, the wisdom of Solomon. If we're going to make chicken spaghetti for dinner, someone needs to pull the meat off this chicken." He pointed to a pale yellow, slippery-looking chicken he'd recently dragged from a pot of boiling water and placed on a plate. "The other will chop onion, green pepper, and garlic."

Noah eyed the repulsive carcass. No way he was touching that. "That's a no-brainer. I'll chop onions."

"Thought you'd say that." The older man chuckled as he handed him a rectangular plastic cutting board, an onion the size of a tennis ball, and a big knife like the chefs used on cooking shows. "The recipe calls for one onion in a quarter-inch dice."

Quarter-inch dice. No problem. Noah placed the board on the counter and the onion on the board. The onion rolled to the edge. He picked it up and repositioned it, only to have it move again. "Tricky little rascal."

Dale stood at his side, watching. "Because you mentioned your inexperience in cooking, I'm going to take the liberty of offering you a few pointers."

Noah nodded in relief. "Okay. Good plan."

"First, you peel the onion. The papery outer layers need to go." Dale expertly nicked the top of the onion with a paring knife, then pulled off a portion of the skin.

"Got it." As instructed, Noah stripped the onion. Pungent fumes wafted under his nose.

"Once it's peeled, you support the onion with your left hand and cut it into slices." The older man turned to give him a warning look. "I don't need to tell you to be careful not to cut yourself. Then you chop the slices into quarter-inch pieces."

Nothing to it. At first, he enjoyed the slicing and chopping. What guy didn't like messing with a big knife? Halfway through the process, the noxious fumes started burning his eyes. Noah blinked hard, forcing cleansing tears, but it didn't put out the fire. He dragged his sleeve across his eyes. Still no relief.

Dale must have noticed his distress. "How's it going over there?"

"Miserably." By now, tears ran down his cheeks. "But I'm almost there."

Another minute or two and he couldn't see past his tears to the cutting board. He put down the knife with a decisive thump. "Done."

Dale came over to inspect his work. "Looks good. I'm impressed."

Noah wiped the moisture from his face with his forearm. "I can do all things through Christ who strengthens me."

His host laughed. "Now I'm doubly impressed. I like a man who can pull out a timely scripture while blinded by an onion." He pointed to the bowl full of chicken pieces he'd stripped from the carcass. "I'm finished here. Do you want me to take over chopping? I can do the pepper and garlic, if you like."

"No, thanks. I committed to the job. I'll finish it." He picked up the green pepper, eyeing it with misgiving. "But warn me now. Is this going to be painful?"

Dale laughed as he patted him on the shoulder. "Walk in the park, son. A walk in the park."

They sat down to dinner almost two hours later. The summer evening sun shone through the sliding door, bathing the little kitchen table in a pool of warm light. Though chicken spaghetti hadn't sounded too appetizing when Dale first mentioned it, the cheesy casserole was surprisingly delicious.

Noah paused, his second forkful halfway to his mouth. "This is good."

Dale smiled. "I always think food tastes better when you've had a part in the preparation."

He chewed up the bite and swallowed. "I'll have to take your word for it. Other than a sandwich or a bowl of cereal, I've never actually made a meal."

Dale reached for the bowl of salad he'd put together while they waited for the spaghetti to bake. "You've lived a very privileged life, Noah."

Noah picked up his glass of tea. "Are you saying that's a bad thing?"

"Not necessarily. I believe God places each one of us where He wants us." Dale served some salad onto his plate. "If there is a downside to privilege, it would be missing out on the common tasks most people perform daily. I believe every experience broadens you, even something simple like preparing a meal, and gives you new insight into the lives of the people you serve. For example, now that you know how much time and tears go into making dinner, you can empathize with a working mother trying to get food on the table for her hungry family after a long day at work."

Noah could definitely see why fast-food restaurants were so popular. "I don't know how they do it. I confess, I've never thought about how difficult it would be."

Dale gave him his gentle smile, filled with grace and acceptance. "You're young and, God willing, you have lots of time to learn. Though I've only known you a couple of days, I can see you have a teachable spirit. There's no limit to what God can do with a heart that's willing to learn and obey."

"You sound like my grandfather. He says the same thing."

The older man nodded. "We heard it from a professor in seminary. Funny how the influence of certain people sticks with us our entire lives."

Noah had a feeling Dale would be that person in his life.

After a few moments of concentrated eating, Dale spoke. "Tell me, how did your visits go today?"

"Better. At least nobody made me sing."

The men shared a laugh over his earlier experience with Dorcas.

Noah put down his fork. "You know what's really weird? How exhausting it is to make all those calls. By the end of my last stop with Edna Mae Jenkins, I was done. Small-talked out. I literally couldn't think of one more word to say. I don't know how you make so many visits each week."

Dale shrugged. "It's more a matter of how could I not do it. The women you've called on these past two days are all widows. Some lost their husbands years ago and some more recently, but all share the same loneliness. I didn't understand how deep and debilitating the sense of loss and isolation can be until I lost my Betty." His ever-present smile disappeared. "It's a dark, all-encompassing feeling I wouldn't wish on my worst enemy."

Just that quickly, he brightened. "So, I make a point to stop by to chat and pray with them."

Noah understood and appreciated his motivation, but it still seemed like a lot of responsibility for one old man. "Why don't their families visit them?"

"Some do, when they can. But others live far away. And everyone is busy. Several of the widows are so old—our friend Dorcas comes to mind—that they've outlived their relatives. They are the last surviving member of their family."

"I don't know. It still doesn't seem right that it falls on you."

Dale smiled. "It's my pleasure. Any service we render to them we do for our Savior. If you recall the story of the good Samaritan, you'll remember Jesus puts a high value on serving our neighbors."

Noah fell silent. The casual conversation was strangely convicting and gave him a lot to think about. Like, what effort had he made to spend time with his grandfather after his grandmother passed away? Honestly, he hadn't given the other man's loneliness a second thought. He'd been so wrapped up in his own life that he'd counted on someone else to take care of his grandfather.

Dale seemed unaware of the serious direction of Noah's thoughts. "Since I didn't see you for lunch, I'm assuming one of the widows fed you."

He shook his head. "They offered, but I'd hit my limit on wrin—uh, racking my brain for something to say, so I had lunch with Emily."

"Aha!" Dale crowed with obvious delight. "Maybe a little matchmaking was a good idea, after all. I can't help thinking you'd make a great team. She could care for the physical needs of the people while you attended to the spiritual. Heart and soul."

Noah lifted a repressive hand as he locked eyes with his host. "Catchy, but no. Really. No. Matchmaking is a terrible idea. Trust me. The doctor and I talked about it. She agrees. We aren't couple material."

"I see." Dale lowered his attention to his plate. "So how was your lunch? I assume you went to Estelle's."

Noah snorted. "Pretty safe bet since it's the only restaurant in town. Actually, it was good. The food was fantastic, and Emily is very easy to talk to."

"I wonder why that is, since you've only known each other two days."

He didn't miss the hopeful tone in the other man's voice. "It's not a romantic thing, if that's what you're suggesting."

"Not at all." Dale lifted his gaze, eyes twinkling. "Just the honest musings of an old man."

An old matchmaker. "It's probably because we're close in age."

His host was clearly skeptical. "Possibly, but experientially you're as different as night and day. Chronology aside, I wouldn't think you two would have any common ground to ease your conversation."

Okay. He had a point. Other than being believers, Noah couldn't think of anything he had in common with the doctor. Still, it wasn't like they had some sort of *soul connection,* despite Dale's implication. "I think she's just a comfortable person. It's difficult to describe, but there's a settledness about her, like if you could see inside her brain, everything would be neat and orderly—no dangling wires or erratic sparks."

Dale frowned and wagged his head. "Not a very romantic picture."

"Exactly. That's what I've been trying to tell you. I would never be able to see her in a romantic way. While she's nice and all, I'm just not attracted to her. But I like her."

"What do you like about her?"

Noah poked at the remaining casserole on his plate. "This is going to sound crazy, but I like that she's not impressed with me. She doesn't care about my job, or my family, or the size of my paycheck. For example, I took her for a ride in my car, at her request, but it was so obvious it was no big deal. She got a kick out of the novelty of it, but I could tell that what I drive has no bearing on what she thinks of me."

Dale raised a brow. "And do those sorts of things matter to the women you date?"

"Well, yeah." Noah shrugged. "They've lived with the best all their lives, so they expect it."

His host frowned. "Does that seem . . . shallow to you?"

Shallow? "I've never thought about it that way before. Yeah, I guess it is. They aren't bad people. I think it goes back to what we talked about earlier. They've been raised in privilege. It's all they know."

"Are you dating anyone special right now?"

"No. I went to dinner with someone last week, but I don't think I'll call her again."

"But you were interested enough to ask her out. So tell me about her."

Noah stared out the window as he brought her image to mind. "Sheridan's beautiful. Tall and slender, blonde hair, brown eyes."

"So far, so good."

Noah laughed. "She's amazing. She leads a singles group on our west campus, has a high-level job at one of the big banks in Houston, her family is well connected . . ."

"Did she like you?"

He shrugged. "She acted like she did."

"But you don't want to ask this paragon out again?"

He'd said that, hadn't he? "I'm probably just being crazy. I'll get home and realize she's the woman for me." He shot Dale a grin. "Be looking for a wedding invitation."

"I'll do that." Dale chuckled. He glanced at Noah's plate. "If you've had enough to eat, I'll get these dishes cleaned up."

"I'm full." Noah placed his napkin on the table and pushed to his feet. "Let me help."

At Dale's surprised look, Noah smiled and shrugged. "Teachable spirit, remember?"

They carried the dishes to the sink, rinsed them, and loaded them into the dishwasher. Noah took charge of wrapping up the leftovers, an especially appealing task once Dale explained it meant dinner was already made for tomorrow night.

After giving the countertops a final wipe-down, the older man turned to him. "Thank you for all your help. I enjoyed the company. I think I'll read for a while, then head off to bed. You're welcome to the television if there's something you'd like to watch."

Noah glanced at the small flat-screen TV on the bookshelf. "I'm not much of a television guy." And he couldn't imagine enjoying anything on a thirty-two-inch screen. "Do you mind if I head over to the church and play the piano for a while?"

"Of course you can." Dale smiled. "I forgot your grandfather said you're a talented musician. The keys to the church are on that hook." He pointed to the strip of wood attached to the wall beside the door. "The light switches for the sanctuary are all on a panel just inside the door on the left. Enjoy yourself. Just be sure to turn off the lights and lock up on your way out."

"Thanks. I will. Good night."

Emily walked the short hall, the slap of her shoes on the tile the only sound in the now-empty clinic. On her way to her office, she stopped to shut off the lights in the exam rooms. As she did every night, she paused in each doorway to admire her clinic. The first two rooms were pretty standard-issue, outfitted for her adult patients, but in the third, she and Jodi and Candy had stenciled brightly colored zoo animals on the walls for their pediatric friends. Each room delighted her.

After all the endless study and preparation, she finally had a practice of her own.

She slipped off her white coat as she entered her office and hung it on a hanger dangling from a hook on the back of the door. Good day today. Each week brought a new patient or two. By the time they'd closed at five, she'd seen ten people. She remembered the scripture in Zechariah that admonished, *Do not despise these small beginnings.*

The clock on the wall opposite her desk said almost eight. She hadn't meant to stay so long. After her staff left at five thirty, she'd hung around to do some reading, and somehow the time got away from her. Ordinarily her stomach would tell her it was quitting time, but after the huge lunch she'd eaten, she wasn't the least bit hungry.

Thinking about lunch with Noah reminded her she'd planned to check on Dale today. She frowned. It seemed odd, worrisome really, that the old man's progress had reversed. Back injuries were tricky to diagnose and treat. Had she missed something?

She could call him and ask how he was feeling, but it'd be best if she ran by his house to see for herself. One of the advantages of rural practices was the feasibility of house calls.

She gathered her handbag from the top drawer of her file cabinet, straightened the brass nameplate on her desk, flipped off the lights, and headed out. Five minutes later she pulled up behind Noah's Tesla in the driveway of the parsonage. She'd expected he'd be here; it wasn't like there were lots of places for him to go, and she was okay with it.

Lunch today went a long way in dispelling her concern there would be awkwardness between them. Since he felt no attraction to her and wasn't aware of hers for him, she had no reason to feel uncomfortable, and with determined neglect, her little crush on him would soon be gone.

For all his outward perfection, Noah was a genuinely nice guy. A bit of a snob, yes, but a fun, considerate one. Their incompatibility didn't mean they couldn't be friends.

Dale answered her knock on the door with a big grin on his face. "Hello there, young lady." He waved her in. "What can I do for you?"

She stopped just inside the threshold. Friend or not, she had no intention of becoming a nuisance. "The question is, what can I do for you? Noah told me your back was giving you more trouble."

He frowned, then dropped his gaze. "I can't say it's giving me more trouble. No. I just felt I should rest it a bit."

She waited until he lifted his eyes to hers. "Be honest with me. Are you in pain?"

He looked away again, this time the task of closing the door occupying his focus. "No pain. Just an occasional twinge."

"You're sure?"

"Let's call it an excess of caution. At my age, one can't be too careful."

Now she was really worried. Dale didn't seem like the type to acknowledge age-related limitations. And why wouldn't he look her in the eye? She reached out, touching him on the arm. "You'd tell me if it was bad, right?"

Finally, he lifted his head and gave her a steady look. "Yes, I would."

"Are you using heat a couple of times a day? Ibuprofen as needed?"

Grinning, he bobbed his head. "Following doctor's orders to the letter."

She laughed. "Thank you for being a model patient." She patted him on the shoulder before taking a step toward the door. "Since you're okay, I'm going to run along."

He stretched out a hand. "Don't go yet. Stay and keep me company."

She shook her head. "I don't want to get in the way. You and Noah—"

"He's not here. He's gone over to the church to play the piano." He paused, and she could practically see the wheels churning in his mind. "His grandfather says he's quite good. I wanted to go over and listen, but I didn't want to tackle the stairs alone. With my bad back and all." He sent her a hopeful, wheedling smile, like the kind she would see on one of her younger brothers when they tried to cadge a treat. "Now that you're here, we can go over together."

How could she resist such a charming request? "I'd be happy to help you with the stairs. When were you planning to go?"

"Right now." He stepped around her, swung open the door, and motioned for her to precede him. "We don't want to miss hearing him play."

At the top of the steps, Emily took his arm, bracing to receive his weight. "You set the pace. I'll follow your lead."

The older man's grip on her arm was strong, but he didn't lean on her as they descended the four stairs. He released her when they reached the bottom. "Thank you so much."

"I don't feel like I did anything."

"Nonsense," he called over his shoulder. "You provided moral support. Sometimes having someone beside you is enough."

She observed him as he walked. She didn't detect any weakness in his stride as he led the way along the narrow sidewalk to the church on the adjacent lot. In fact, she had to hurry to keep up. Maybe it was just as he said. He was being a little extra cautious.

The sounds of classical music carried in the air as they approached the sanctuary.

"He *is* good." Dale pulled open the unlocked door and waited for her to enter.

Shaking her head, she backed up a step. "No. This is as far as I'm going." She waved as she turned to leave. "Enjoy the concert."

"But, but . . . how will I get home?"

She frowned. "I'm sure Noah will be happy to provide moral support on the stairs for the return trip."

"I'm sure he would. But I'd hate to ask him to stop playing to escort me home. You young people keep later hours than us old folks." He must have caught a glimpse of her indecision. "We'll only stay for a song or two," he cajoled.

The desire to serve warred with the need for self-preservation. She needed to wean herself from her little infatuation with Noah. And she didn't want to appear to be stalking him. How would it look for her to show up at his private concert?

"Please?"

One look into the older man's pleading eyes, and she was sunk. How could she say no to that? She sighed. "Okay. But just two songs."

The lights were on in the sanctuary, and Dale insisted on walking to the front of the room, dashing her hopes that they could slip into the back and listen to the concert undetected.

"Oh, hey." Noah lifted his hands from the keys when he saw them in the aisle. "What's going on?"

Dale stopped mid-trek. "We wanted to hear you play."

We? Wait just a minute. This was one hundred percent his idea. However, since contradicting the pastor would only make an awkward situation worse, she settled for a sheepish wave before dropping onto the nearest pew.

The good-natured smile on Noah's face said he took their intrusion with grace. "Any requests?"

Dale didn't stop until he was at the front pew. "Whatever you're doing sounds great."

Major understatement. Noah played the complex piece with musicality and power.

Nodding, he returned his attention to the keys, picking up where he'd left off.

Disregarding the acute discomfort of invading his private time, Emily admitted watching Noah at the piano was pure pleasure. And not just because of his looks. Joy radiated from his face as his fingers danced over the keys. Here was a man doing what he loved.

All too soon the piece came to a close. As the last note drifted off, she and Dale erupted into spontaneous applause.

"I didn't know the old piano could sound so good," Dale said.

Noah looked up, his expression pleased and somewhat surprised, as though he'd forgotten they were in the room. "Thank you. Who's next? Emily, do you play?"

She shook her head no as Dale nodded the affirmative.

Noah laughed. "Looks like you two need to get your stories straight."

Dale swiveled around to face her. "When we were talking the other day, you told me you liked to play the piano to relax."

Why did he have to have such a good memory? "I did say that, but I don't play like . . . that." She pointed helplessly to the maestro at the piano.

"You're being modest." Noah waved her forward. "Come on, Dr. Cutler, show us what you've got."

Another, stronger headshake. "Not modest, no. Honest. Honest Emily here. Ask anyone."

Noah laughed. "You may as well come up here and play because now that I know you do, I won't rest until I hear you."

Her heart sank with the grim assurance he spoke the truth. He wouldn't leave her alone until she answered his challenge. She pushed to her feet, stepped around the end of the pew, and trudged up to the piano, once again horribly aware she was way out of her league with this man.

Noah scooted over on the bench and patted the empty spot he'd just vacated. "Have a seat."

Oh boy. His proximity would *not* boost her mediocre skill level. She slid onto the bench, careful not to bump his hip with her own. "I don't think I can use—"

She felt her jaw drop as she looked at the empty music shelf. The look she sent him was pure shock. "You played without music? You have that entire piece memorized?"

He shrugged. "Yeah. But I bet we can find something here for you to use."

"How about a hymnal?" Ever-helpful Dale tossed out the suggestion.

There was no way to back out gracefully. "Sure. That'll work."

Noah retrieved the red-covered hymnal from the chair Dale used to preach from on Sunday and handed it to her. Instead of stepping down to sit beside Dale, he returned to the bench and sat.

Oh boy. Oh boy. As she flipped through the book, looking for something without too many sharps or flats, she felt the eyes of both men upon her. She wasn't surprised when the first chortle escaped.

Noah tilted his head toward hers. "What's so funny?"

Nothing. She'd probably never been in a less funny position in her life. Turning slightly, she met his eyes for a moment, then sighed and dropped her gaze. "I laugh when I'm nervous."

In the silence following her confession, she could feel him studying her. "Nuh-uh. Really?"

She nodded. And giggled. "Really."

"What's there to be nervous about?" The man to whom everything seemed to come easily sounded genuinely puzzled. "It's just Dale and me. You're among friends."

What a nice thing to say. And it was true. Of course, it would be easier if one of the friends wasn't a perfect specimen of manhood who also happened to be an extraordinary pianist. Still, the tickle in her throat subsided.

"Here's one." She propped the hymnal on the music ledge, took a deep breath, and plunged in. After the first couple of sluggish measures, she found her rhythm. By focusing on the century-old lyrics and familiar tune, she successfully blocked out the terrific-smelling distraction beside her. Mostly.

She played the first stanza and chorus then folded her hands in her lap.

Dale clapped.

Noah nudged her. "That was great. You're not stopping, are you? Come on. Pick another one."

She shook her head. Her playing wasn't great, but at least she hadn't embarrassed herself. A wise woman quit while she was ahead. "I don't think—"

"Come on. We'll play one together." Without waiting for her assent, Noah snatched up the hymnal, flipped several pages, and replaced it on the ledge. "You take the treble clef; I'll take the bass."

He scooted over a couple of inches until their bodies were touching, his warm hip settling against hers. "Start when you're ready. I'll catch up."

It took a moment of concentrated effort to retrieve her thoughts from his lovely scent and their physical connection and focus them on the printed page. Left hand in her lap, she picked out the notes with her right. As she carried the simple melody, Noah played the notes of the bass clef, embellishing the written score and enhancing the overall effect.

"Wow. You make me sound good."

"You *are* good." He leaned toward her to whisper, "If Dale had any sense, he'd fire that horrendous woman who plays everything half-tempo and hire you. Are you interested in moonlighting on weekends as a pianist?"

The intimacy of their positions infused breathlessness into her laughter.

"Bravo." Dale clapped. "You two make a great team. How about another song?"

Emily pushed to her feet and nodded toward Noah. "Go ahead."

He caught her arm and pulled her back to the bench. "No way. If I have to perform, then so do you."

They played through three more favorites, ending the last with a burst of shared laughter.

"That was fun." Emily looked to Dale for his reaction. His pew was empty. "Where's Dale?"

Noah followed the line of her gaze and frowned. "I don't know. I didn't see him get up."

She hadn't either. She'd been too caught up in the music, or more accurately, her accompanist. "It's hard to believe he went back to the house alone. He told me he didn't like to take the stairs without help."

Noah turned to her, brows lifted. "Dale said that?"

Sharing a bench to play a duet was close. Sharing a bench to talk was too close. With their faces mere inches apart, she could describe in detail the pigmentation of his irises or the spot above his upper lip where he hadn't shaved as closely. The snug arrangement seemed more suited to kissing than talking.

Kissing! Heat flooded her face.

"Yes." Without being obvious, she shifted away to create space between them so she could think without distraction. "I dropped by tonight to check on him after you mentioned he wasn't himself this morning. When I got ready to leave, he asked me to walk him down the stairs. He said he wasn't comfortable on them without help."

Noah frowned. "That's weird."

"I thought so too. Especially when he took my arm coming down the stairs and then didn't lean on me at all. When we got here and I told him I was leaving, he insisted I stay to walk him back."

His frown deepened. "He's pretty old. Think he's getting senile?"

"Not that I've observed. I haven't known him long, but he seems super sharp with details." She paused. "I wonder if he was more shaken by his back injury than he let on. That would explain his sudden cautiousness. He's trying to prevent a recurrence."

Noah's gaze returned to the empty pew. "So where is he?"

"Good question." She swung her legs around the end of the bench and stood. "I'll go look for him."

He pushed to his feet. "I'll come with you."

"No." She held out a hand to stop him. "Stay and play. I didn't mean to interrupt you."

"I'm done." He hopped up and circled to her side. "And I'm not letting you walk in the dark all by yourself."

"That's very chivalrous of you. Think there's bad guys out there?"

He snorted. "No self-respecting bad guy would be caught dead this far from civilization. But coyotes, now that's a different story."

While she was pretty sure he was kidding about the coyotes, she wasn't taking any chances. She waited close beside him while he locked up. Security lights mounted on the corners of the building illuminated the surrounding area to near daylight. No predators. No Dale. They followed the wide sidewalk around the front of the church to where it intersected a narrower one leading across the grassy lot to the parsonage. Even in the stretch of semidarkness between the lights of the church and the porch light at Dale's, it was obvious they were alone.

"No sign of him." Emily frowned. "I guess he went in."

"Looks like it."

The evening was warm, with only a slight breeze to stir the sultry air. Overhead, thousands of stars glittered in the cloudless sky. An unseen orchestra of crickets played a shrill serenade as they strolled along the path to the parsonage. Suddenly the insect chorus reached a crescendo, filling the night with a swelling sound.

Noah paused to stare into the field. "Those are some seriously noisy bugs."

She smiled. "Sounds like summer. I'm sure you have crickets in Houston."

"Yes, but ours are more refined."

They laughed.

All too soon, they were at the house. "This is my stop." Emily halted in the driveway beside her car. "Do you mind texting me when you get inside, so I'll know Dale made it in okay?"

"No problem." Noah pulled his cell phone from his pocket. "Give me your number."

After they exchanged information, she opened the car door and slid behind the wheel. "Thank you for walking me back. And I'm sorry about interrupting your evening tonight."

"Are you kidding? I'm glad you came. Really, Doc. It was fun."

Emily hadn't made it back to her apartment when her phone dinged with a text. *Dale's here. Sound asleep in his recliner.*

She replied with a smiley face.

CHAPTER SIX

Noah steadied the paper bag on the passenger seat as he bumped and lurched along the gravel road. He didn't know whether the city, county, or state was responsible for maintaining the crater-pocked street, but somebody needed to get out here and fix it. Since he was stuck in Village Green for a few more days, he might as well make some calls.

He pulled into Mrs. Palmer's equally treacherous driveway and parked.

She waited on the porch for him. "Right on time," she called as he climbed out of the car.

"Yes, ma'am. Didn't want to be late with your lunch." Bag in hand, he took the stairs cautiously, stepping around the most-rotted wood.

She met him at the top, arms held wide. "It's so nice to see you again, Preacher Man."

It didn't seem polite to mention he was only back because she made him.

Bending, he gathered her into a one-armed hug. Beneath her faded cotton dress, the old woman felt fragile, mostly skin and bones. Considering her feisty personality, he'd expected her to be more substantial.

She opened the door and the stuffy *old* smell he'd begun to associate with the citizens of Village Green wafted from the house. "Come on in. I've got the table all ready."

He followed her through the shadows, down the short hall, and into her kitchen. As with every surface in the parts of the house he'd seen, Dorcas's kitchen was piled with stuff. At her small round table covered with a green vinyl cloth, she'd pushed aside the stacks of mail and an army of pill bottles and set the cleared spot with places for two. The china plates, patterned with faint pink blossoms, looked antique, probably the ones she'd collected as a new bride. A mason jar with three yellow blooms sat in the center. She'd obviously gone to a lot of trouble.

"Dorc—, I mean, Esther, this looks very festive," he said.

She nodded regally. "Thank you. It's not often I have company at meals. I usually eat in front of the television."

Something inside him shifted painfully. He thought of Dale's words the other night when he described the deep sense of loss and isolation he'd experienced after losing his wife. At the time, Noah had thought he could relate. The few days he'd spent in Village Green, without his friends and customary round of activities, had left him feeling lonely. Suddenly he could see what he *suffered* was merely inconvenience, a slight discomfort for a limited time, while this woman lived in true isolation, day in and day out.

She gestured toward the table. "Sit yourself down."

"No, ma'am. You sit and let me serve you."

He pulled out her chair, and she settled in with a contented sigh. "I feel just like Queen Esther."

Noah opened the bag he'd set on the counter and pulled out several containers. He removed the plastic lid and steam curled into the air as he placed the first, still-hot dish on the table. "Here's the chicken. When I told Estelle I was bringing lunch to you, she insisted on sending coleslaw and potato salad. She said they were your favorites."

Dorcas clasped her hands over her heart. "Isn't it the sweetest thing that she remembered?"

Noah added the two extra containers to the table and lifted off the lids.

She pointed a gnarled finger toward a drawer in the cabinets. "Go ahead and get us a couple of serving spoons before you sit down, will you?"

After they'd eaten their fill, Dorcas sat back with a sigh and laid her napkin on the table. "That was a fine meal."

Noah nodded. "Estelle certainly knows her way around a frying pan."

"That's the truth." She stuck her finger in her mouth, apparently trying to dislodge something from a molar. "How did you know I liked fried chicken?"

Horrified, he averted his eyes. "I mentioned to Dr. Cutler that I was coming out here for lunch, and she said you were a big fan."

"I like that Dr. Cutler." She paused, presumably for more digging. "At first, I wasn't sure what I thought about a woman doctor. We didn't have them in my day. But I like her. She's mighty smart and real friendly. It'll be good to have a medical person here in town again."

He risked another look at her. Happily, her hands were in her lap. "There are no other physicians in Village Green?"

She shook her head, white curls bobbing. "We had one a while back. Dr. Tucker. Good man. When he retired, nobody wanted to take his place. So if we need a clinic, we drive into Corsicana. They've got a hospital there too."

Coming from Houston where there was a doctor, hospital, or clinic on practically every corner, he couldn't imagine living somewhere without direct access to medical care. Village Green was as close to *Little House on the Prairie* as he wanted to be.

"Why would anyone choose to live here?" The rhetorical question was out of his mouth before he could stop it.

Rather than take offense, Dorcas laughed. "I 'spect to a fancy man like you, our town feels like the end of the earth."

Fancy man? That didn't sound like a compliment.

"Back in the day, Village Green offered everything a body could want. We had a doctor, and a dentist, and a real nice dress shop."

He thought of all the boarded-up buildings along Main Street. "What happened?"

"The interstate came through a couple miles from here and took all the traffic and business with it. Folks moved away."

Understandable. He'd have been on the first bus out of here. "Why did you stay?"

"I've lived here my whole life." She lifted bony shoulders in a philosophical shrug. "Where would I go?"

Just about anywhere else would be an improvement.

"Fact is, even without the doctors and shops, we've got things you big city folks don't have."

As if. He leaned back in his chair, folded his arms across his chest, and lifted his chin in challenge. "Name one."

She met his eyes. "Peace and quiet. Places to stretch out."

"Okay, I agree, you have that in abundance."

"It's my opinion that when folks live slower, they live better. Got more time for each other and the things that matter."

That must be what people who had nothing to do told themselves to feel better about their miserable existence. "If you say so."

"You seem like a smart fellow, Preacher Man. You'll figure it out."

Palms on the table for leverage, she pushed to her feet. "Let me get these dishes done so we can do a little singing before you go."

Oh no. Not the singing. He glanced at his watch. He'd been there over an hour, the unofficial length of time Dale suggested for a visit. Duty done. He could excuse himself with a clear conscience.

But then she'd be alone again.

"Here, let me help you." He stood and scooped the plates from the table.

Hands on hips, she sent him a look of admiration. "Good-looking and handy in the kitchen too? The women must be swarming you."

He didn't tell her that he'd only recently done his first dish. Or that the women he knew wouldn't be impressed with his newfound talent since they didn't do dishes either.

After they'd cleaned up and packed the leftovers in the refrigerator, Dorcas led them to the sitting room.

Picking up the hymnal on the table, he took his spot on the chair across from the piano. "What do you want to start with?"

They ran through three songs in their caterwauling style before Noah had sung all he could. He replaced the hymnal on the table and stood. "That was fun, but it's time for me to go."

She turned toward him. "That's a da—er . . . darn shame. Have you decided how long you're going to be in town?"

"Looks like I'm going to be here another week."

Not by choice. Due to Dale's stalled recovery, his grandfather had asked him to stick around a little longer. To be certain his dear friend recovered fully before leaving him alone. After his many protests fell on deaf ears, Noah finally, begrudgingly, had agreed to one more week.

Dorcas flashed him a smile of recently-picked-clean, crooked yellow teeth. "I'm glad to hear it. We have time for another visit. Next time, I'll fix you my tuna."

Emily's warning about the cat food flashed through his mind. "No!" He lowered his voice. "What I mean is, next time I'll take you out. Sure. We can have lunch at Estelle's."

How did he get himself into this mess?

Noah steered his car toward town. He didn't want to stay another week, and he didn't want to take an old woman who picked her teeth at the table out to lunch. On the other hand, he didn't want to face her tuna, either.

Without conscious thought, he pulled into the clinic parking lot, parked beside the doctor's old Honda, and walked in.

"Hello, Pastor Speers." The receptionist left the words *Back again?* unspoken, but he heard them just the same.

Both hands on the counter, he leaned in. "Hey, has your boss got any free time this afternoon?"

"Do you need a medical appointment?"

Why did she keep asking him that? Did he look sick? "No, I just want to talk with her."

She glanced at her computer screen. "She's with a patient right now. After that she has an opening."

"I'll take it."

"Fine." She typed something, then sent him a smile. "If you'll have a seat, they'll call you back when she's ready."

For the second time in a week, he found himself pacing the small waiting room. He studied the artwork, perused the magazine titles, and noted the new growth on the plant by the window. Ten minutes after he arrived, the inner door opened, and white-coated Emily emerged with her patient.

"Goodbye, Mrs. Nelson. Candy, the receptionist, will schedule you for a recheck in a month. If you need us before then, don't hesitate to call."

"Thank you, Doctor."

"My pleasure. Take care."

After sending Mrs. Nelson off with a pat on the back and a smile, Emily turned to him, surprise on her face. "Hello, Noah. What can I do for you?"

Last night's piano partner looked all business in her lab coat with her long hair pulled back in a tidy bun. He felt a little silly under her clear-eyed gaze. He didn't know why he'd stopped. She was obviously busy, and he had friends at home he could call. He shook his head. "I shouldn't have come in the middle of your workday. It was thoughtless—"

She waved off his concern. "Don't be ridiculous. I'm never too busy to talk with a friend. Come on back and tell me what's going on."

He followed her through the door and down the tiled hall to her cramped little office. She waited for him to enter, gesturing toward the wooden chairs in front of her desk, before closing the door behind them.

She pointed to the tall Styrofoam cup on the edge of the desk. "Jodi just brought me a Dr Pepper from Estelle's. I haven't taken a drink yet. Do you want me to find an extra cup so we can split it?"

"No, thanks." He settled into a chair. "You enjoy it. I just finished lunch with Dorcas."

Her face lit as she peeled the paper off her straw and inserted it into the lid. "Ah, that's right. You two had a date. How was it?"

"I took your advice and brought fried chicken. She was thrilled."

Instead of sitting behind the desk, she propped on the corner facing him, her slender legs crossed at the ankles. She sent him a look of warm approval. "That was really nice of you."

If she'd told him a week ago that he was nice, he'd have agreed. Absolutely. Noah Speers was a real standup guy. Just ask anyone. Today, he knew himself a little better, and suddenly he wasn't so sure. "No, it was strictly self-preservation."

Her eyes danced as she laughed. Why hadn't he noticed how pretty she was? "The food, maybe, but not the luncheon. I know she enjoyed your company."

He thought about the delighted look on Dorcas's wrinkled face when he arrived, the special plates and flowers on the table. "Yeah. She seemed happy to see me. She invited me back to lunch next week for her famous tuna, and before I knew what I was saying, I told her I'd take her out to lunch."

Her thick brows lifted. "I thought you were leaving."

"Me too." He pushed out of his chair, too antsy to sit. "I made the mistake of telling my grandfather how weird Dale was acting, and he pressured me into staying another week to keep an eye on him." He paced the small area behind the chairs. "So, I'm stuck in no-man's-land for another seven days."

She tilted her head to study him. "What bothers you the most? The delay or the lunch date?"

He stopped, her perceptiveness bringing a smile to his face. He liked that in the short time they'd known each other, she got him. "It's pretty much a tie. I'm so ready to get back to my life and my work. This was supposed to be a couple of days, not a life sentence. And honestly, I can't think of anything a whole lot worse than dining out with a woman who digs in her mouth after she eats."

Emily nodded in commiseration. "I can't help you with your extended stay. That's up to you and Dale and your grandfather. But I can offer to join you and Dorcas for lunch. There's not much I can do about her picking her teeth, but I can help carry the burden of conversation if you like."

"Would you do that?" A grin split his face. For the first time that day, things were looking up. "Aw, man. Doc, you're a lifesaver."

She hadn't planned on saving Noah's life today. Or seeing him, for that matter. Knowing he was leaving town, she hadn't hoped to cross paths with him again. When she discovered him in her waiting room, her first thought, once she'd recovered from the surprise, was that he'd come to say goodbye.

Despite his disappointment in cooling his heels another week in Village Green, she was elated. Not that she was looking for romance. She wasn't foolish enough to harbor hope that he'd fall for her over the next week, or ever, but knowing they'd meet for lunch gave her a treat to look forward to. Noah was fun. They had fun together. Practical Emily was too realistic to ask for more.

She hopped off the desk and circled around to her computer. "Do you know when you're doing lunch? I'll block it out on my calendar."

"We didn't make a firm commitment." He returned to the chair where he'd started and sat. "Since you're the one with patients, why don't you tell me what's convenient for you?"

Slipping into her seat, she opened her laptop and accessed the appointment schedule for next week. "So far Wednesday looks light. I can block off between eleven and one."

"Great. I'll call Dorcas when I leave here and tell her we're on for Wednesday at eleven." He leaned forward, locking eyes with her. "I really owe you for this."

She shook her head. "You don't owe me a thing. I'm happy to do it."

"You say that now. Let's see how happy you are when she starts fishing around in her mouth with her finger."

She laughed.

He suddenly sobered, his eyes searching her face. "Why are you here?"

Sensing there was more to his question, but not certain what he was asking, she shrugged. "Because the clinic doesn't close until five?"

He frowned. "I'm not asking about today specifically. My question is, why would an intelligent, attractive woman bury herself in a place like Village Green?"

She filed away the intelligent, attractive part to savor later. "My medical school at TBU offers a program in which a doctor agrees to practice in an underserved area in exchange for the cancellation of their student debt."

He picked up the engraved nameplate from her desk and turned it over in his hands. "I guess medical school is pretty pricey."

She nodded. "It was for my family. I'm the oldest of four kids. That's a lot of people for a teacher and an auto mechanic to educate."

"Still, couldn't you have signed on with a hospital or clinic in a nice metropolitan area and paid off your loan with your salary? Avoid the whole indentured-servant thing?"

"I suppose so. But I wanted to serve. This program seemed like the best way to connect me with people who need me. And I actually *like* Village Green."

He replaced the nameplate on the desk to give her his full attention. "What do you like about it?" He sounded genuinely perplexed.

"Let me see . . ." Her feelings for her new home were difficult to put into words. "I like on-street parking without meters. I like that the bank serves fresh muffins and juice every day, and that when I step inside everybody there greets me by name. I like that I can walk from my apartment—"

"So you're into the whole small-town thing."

She nodded. "I'm from a small town, so yeah."

"And you don't miss all the amenities—like decent stores, salons, or any traces of culture or civilization?"

She could tell by his expression he was truly trying to understand. "Not really. And I know if I did need to make the occasional trip to a store or salon, I could hop in my car and be somewhere in under an hour. Factoring in traffic, I bet you couldn't do much better in Houston."

"You have a point." He lifted his gaze to hers. "But what about dating?"

For a heart-stopping split second, she thought he was asking her out. "Wh—what about it?"

"I assume that one day you'd like to meet someone and marry. Maybe even have a family."

So it had been a hypothetical question. Her stuttering heart found its regular rhythm.

"Sure."

"Where are you going to find someone around here? You deserve better than an uneducated redneck."

She sent him a disapproving frown. "I've met many educated people here in Village Green."

His raised brow challenged her. "Young? Single?"

"Well, no." Before he could elaborate on his depressing point, she lifted her chin and added, "I've always believed when the time was right, God would bring the right man to me."

"To Village Green?" Noah snorted. "Good luck with that. He'll have to import an out-of-towner since there's nobody even marginally eligible around here."

"I believe He's able."

Silence settled between them. Finally, Noah spoke. "Do you think I'm shallow?"

The random question tempted her to laugh, but the earnest look on his handsome face said he was serious. She studied her hands while she formulated a response. He was a snob, certainly, but shallow? At last, she lifted her gaze to him. "Honestly Noah, I don't know you well enough to answer that."

His full-bodied laugh caught her off guard.

"What's so funny?"

His eyes twinkled with mirth. "I knew you'd say something like that. That you wouldn't brush off the question with a socially acceptable 'of course not.' You're so honest."

She was glad he made it sound like a good thing. "Aren't your friends honest with you?"

"That depends. I've known a couple of guys my whole life who'd probably shoot straight with me. To a point. And my family would be honest with me, except they're biased in my favor. Most of the people I know through church would tell me what I wanted to hear."

"They treat you like a celebrity."

He stiffened, as though the idea repelled him. "No!"

After a thoughtful pause, he shifted. "Well, maybe a little." Another pause. Another self-conscious shift. "Okay, they do. A lot. But I don't think of myself as a celebrity. And I hope I don't act like one." The wince that followed told her he remembered a time or two when he had.

"My grandfather started the church with twenty people on folding chairs in an abandoned warehouse. Between him and my dad, they've built one of the largest churches in the country. They are revered. As the son and heir apparent, I think it's fair to say some of that trickles down to me."

She nodded. "So, people are more likely to try to please you than to tell you the truth?"

"Yeah." He narrowed his eyes at her. "Do they teach you this stuff in medical school?"

"I beg your pardon?"

"I'm thirty years old and haven't done this much introspection in . . . ever. Do you have this weird I-need-to-search-my-soul effect on everyone?"

She laughed. "Not that I'm aware of."

The tension he'd arrived with no longer showed on his face when he smiled. "I didn't plan to come by your office today. To be honest, I'm not sure why I stopped. I was so frustrated after I spoke to my grandfather this morning. I didn't see another week here coming. Then when Dorcas found out about my extended stay and invited me to lunch again, I couldn't say no and I couldn't eat her tuna, so I ended up asking her to lunch. From the time I first drove into town, I've been asking God to show me what He's doing, but all I see are delays from other people dictating my life."

"I'm sorry, Noah."

"As I drove away from her place, it all came to a head, and I just wanted to talk it out. The weirdest part is, it never occurred to me to call anyone from home. It's like I knew they wouldn't understand." He lifted his eyes to hers for a long, searching look. "And you would."

After a weighted pause, he gave her his familiar grin and got to his feet. "Anyway, sorry for dropping in on you. Again. I know I'm driving your receptionist nuts. I really appreciate you seeing me."

She stood as well. "You're welcome. But I didn't do anything."

"You did. I can't explain it, but after talking to you, I always feel better. Calmer." He made a stirring motion over his chest. "It's like all the agitation brewing in there has stilled. You're a human tranquilizer."

Just what every woman wanted to hear. "I'm glad I could help."

"I'll leave you to your next patient. Thanks, Doc. See you Sunday." With a wink and a wave, he let himself out.

Emily continued to stare at the door long after he'd gone.

Wow. If she was a human tranquilizer, he was a double shot of espresso. Energy pulsed off of him in waves. Being with him made her feel supercharged, like she'd just downed a Big Gulp of Dr Pepper.

There was a tap on the door, and Jodi popped her head in. "Dr. Cutler, I just brought your patient to Exam 2."

"Thanks, Jodi. I'm coming."

Picking up the tablet from the rack outside the room, Emily opened the chart, scanning for the patient's information and chief complaint: Seventy-two-year-old male. Arthur Dyson. Headache. Stuffy nose.

She swung open the door of the exam room and stepped inside. "Hello, Mr. Dyson. I'm Dr. Cutler."

"Howdy, Doctor." After shaking her hand, he pointed to the woman at his side. "This is my missus."

"Mrs. Dyson, it's a pleasure to meet you."

"We're grateful you can see us," the woman said. "Poor Arthur's been feeling bad. Of course, being a man, he didn't want to come to the doctor."

He sent Emily an apologetic look. "It wasn't that I didn't want to, exactly. Just don't need a doctor for a cold. I've been telling the wife here I'm fine."

"If you're fine, then why have you been moping around the house for days?"

Emily took a seat on the stool opposite them. "Sometimes it's good to come in just to check things out. Mr. Dyson, why don't you tell me what's going on?"

"It started with a cold—" his wife began.

"She asked me to tell it." He glared at his wife before turning to Emily. "It started with a cold."

She bit back a smile as she made notes on the tablet. "How long ago was that?"

"A week and a half. Maybe two weeks. It seemed like it was getting better. My nose wasn't hardly runny, then it got all stuffy again."

"His mucus is green," Mrs. Dyson reported.

Another glare. "I'm telling it."

"Have you taken anything for the congestion?" Emily asked.

His wife snorted. "As if you could get a man to take medicine."

Emily slid off the stool to wash her hands at the small sink. "Hop up on the table and let's take a look, shall we?"

She fitted the otoscope to his ear. The tympanic membrane was cloudy due to fluid, but not red. No infection.

"If you're looking for brains, I'm not sure you'll find any," he quipped.

"Based on my initial findings, I'd say you have a wonderful, fully functioning brain." She gently inserted the otoscope into his nostrils. Turbinates were swollen and red.

"Let's take a peek into your mouth, please." A river of cloudy gunk flowed down the back of his throat. She tossed the tongue depressor into the trash.

She tapped his maxillary sinuses. "When you came in, you mentioned a headache. How is it if I touch it here?"

He winced. "Sore. Even makes my teeth ache."

After feeling his lymph nodes, she put the stethoscope in her ears. "I'm going to listen to your heart and lungs."

His heartbeat was strong and regular. She moved behind him and listened at several locations on his lower back. Lungs clear.

She draped the stethoscope around her neck and crossed to the sink to rewash her hands. "Mr. Dyson, you have a sinus infection."

His wife shot him a look of triumph. "I told you."

Before they could start squabbling again, Emily asked, "Are you allergic to any medications?"

"No, ma'am."

"Good. We'll start you on a round of antibiotics. Once you've taken the medication for a day or two, you'll start feeling better, but you must finish the entire dose to be sure we knocked out the infection completely."

Mrs. Dyson accepted the assignment with a martial gleam in her eye. "I'll make sure he takes it."

After electronically sending his prescription to the pharmacy, Emily stood. "This should take care of it, but if something comes up, or if you have any questions, please give us a call."

Mr. Dyson scooted off the exam table. "Thanks, Doc."

She herded the couple down the hall and through the door leading out into the waiting room. "It was a pleasure to meet you both. Take care."

A text message from her landlord popped up on her cell phone shortly after she'd seen her last patient for the day.

Don't forget the softball game tomorrow at 9:30 at the Green.

She *had* forgotten. The day she'd moved into her apartment, Joe and his wife had asked if she was interested in playing softball for the town league. It sounded like they always needed extra players to fill out the holes in their roster. She'd accepted the invitation—she was a pretty decent ballplayer, and it would give her another way to interact with her Village Green neighbors.

Her thoughts went immediately to Noah. Since he would be in town, maybe he'd like to come. Sure. Why not? It wasn't as if she was trying to finagle more time with him. She simply wanted to offer him entertainment while he was stuck here. She texted him an invitation and the details before she could talk herself out of it.

CHAPTER SEVEN

Emily loved her apartment. The two-bedroom, bath-and-a-half flat overlooking the Green was head and shoulders above any place she'd ever lived. Soaring twelve-foot ceilings, hardwood floors, and ornate crown molding gave a nod to the history of the building, while the sparkling white kitchen with top-of-the-line appliances, and the pristine bathrooms outfitted with lots of gleaming white marble and new plumbing, firmly grounded the space in the present.

The fact she lived there rent-free was an unlooked-for bonus. Apparently, the good people of Village Green recognized the need to sweeten the deal if they were to attract a doctor to town. Her landlord, Joe Wolfe, owned the historic, block-long brick building across from the park and built apartments on the second story, above the shops. When the city was in negotiations with the doctor-placement program, he volunteered the use of one of his spaces to anyone agreeing to set up their practice in town.

Emily met Joe and his beautiful wife, Eden, the day she moved in. Every mile closer to town had weighed more heavily on her heart that day. Had she made a mistake in following the leading to serve the underserved when her friends from medical school had all taken jobs in prosperous communities? As the old state highway led her farther from the familiar, she'd wondered if she'd misheard God. After all, her friends were still serving, just without the sacrifice.

As she pulled into the parking lot, her father, driving behind her in the rental truck crammed with all her earthly possessions, and her mother, bringing up the rear in the family car so her parents could return home that night, pulled in behind her. Emily saw a small group gathered by the apartment door. Once she and her parents had parked and emerged from their vehicles, the group approached, a movie-star-pretty couple leading the delegation.

"Hey! Are you Dr. Emily Cutler?" The guy extended his hand. "I'm Joe Wolfe."

His wife had not been so formal. No sooner had Emily confirmed her identity than Eden swept her into a hug. "Welcome to Village Green. We are so glad you're here."

Behind her, the other thirty-somethings waited to add their warm greetings. By the time Emily crawled exhausted into her bed that night, all her nerves and misgivings over her new assignment had disappeared. God had faithfully led her to a place of service and blessing.

Now, pushing aside the heavy, cream-colored drapes at her bedroom window, she looked out at the park across the street. People had already begun to gather at the softball field.

She pressed her nose to the pane. From this distance, it was impossible to tell if Noah was among them. His text last night thanked her for the invitation but hadn't said whether he would join them.

She released the curtain, letting the fabric swish back into place. If he showed up, great. If he didn't, that was fine too. She would enjoy herself whether he came or not.

Last night, she'd doubled down on her determination not to get too attached to him. She'd been understandably flattered when he'd sought her out yesterday, more so that he seemed to genuinely value her opinion. And she really did like him. He was funny, self-deprecating, and very real beneath his too-good-to-be-true looks.

But besides being out of her league—*way out*—he was leaving. Two very good reasons to keep her head on straight.

Grabbing her sneakers from the closet, she sat on the end of the bed to put them on. She ducked into the bathroom to apply a layer of sunscreen before grabbing her ball cap, tucking her keys and water bottle into her handbag, and heading out.

Her apartment exited at the rear of the building. She followed the sidewalk to the end of the block, made the corner, crossed Main Street between the pedestrian lines, and entered the Green at an opening in the black, wrought-iron fence.

Hot sunshine beat down on her as she made her way to the baseball diamond. The forecast said they'd make a hundred degrees today. Someone told her they usually played their games on Sunday afternoon, but in the oppressive heat of summer they scheduled them early Saturday morning.

"Hey, Emily." Hallie Gunther broke from the gathered group and trotted over to her, a big smile on her face. "Glad you could make it. I'm keeping score today, so we're down at least one player."

Emily had met Hallie the night she moved in and liked her instantly. Similarly aged, with many common interests, they were sure to be the best of friends. "You're not playing?" Concerned, she studied her face. "Everything okay?"

"Yes." Hallie briefly placed her hand on her abdomen as she glanced over her shoulder at two fast-approaching women before turning back to Emily to whisper, "I'll come by to see you on Monday, and we'll talk."

"Good."

"Hey, Emily!" Eden, gorgeous even in a baggy T-shirt and cut-offs, caught her in a hug. "How've you been?"

"Great. Business is picking up at the clinic. I have you to thank for putting in a good word for me."

"Are you kidding? You're amazing. What a blessing to bring Jake to you when we need a doctor, instead of driving to Corsicana."

Eden's adorable two-year-old son had been one of her first patients. "How is he?"

"He's good. My mother-in-law has him this morning. His rash is completely gone, thanks to you." Eden's smiled dimmed. "We just started potty training, so we're spending most of our time in the bathroom."

"Bless your heart." Emily gave her a look of commiseration before turning to the newly married first-grade teacher standing on her other side. "How are you, Riley? Have you started school?"

The pretty brunette nodded. "We've had our teacher in-service. The kids start back on Monday."

"And so it begins. Are you ready?"

She shrugged. "Yes and no. I really love teaching, but it's been fun to have a couple months at home being a newlywed."

Though Riley had married the most recently, Emily knew all three of the friends had tied the knot within the last year. So much for Noah's concerns about dating prospects in Village Green. These women all found someone wonderful here.

Of course, none of them was quite as wonderful as Noah. Emily excised the thought as a surgeon would a cancerous tumor.

Noah might be everything a girl could ask for, but this girl wasn't asking.

The foursome walked back toward the others, joining them at the rickety, three-bench bleacher on what appeared to be the home team's side. The corresponding bleacher on the opposite side of the field sat empty.

"Hey, Emily, thanks for coming out." Sam Walker, Riley's husband and a local cop, clapped her on the back. "Infield or outfield?"

"I don't have a preference. Wherever you need me is fine."

"You've got some experience, right?"

She nodded.

"Let's put her in right field for now." Hallie's husband, Trey, who served with Sam as cocaptain for the team, filled names into a template. He glanced at her. "You may have to do some extra running if Cyrus doesn't make it."

Sam frowned. "I forgot to tell you he texted me while I was unloading the equipment from my truck. He won't be here. He's got to work this morning."

Trey pushed up the brim of his hat to scratch his forehead. "I was afraid of that."

Apparently, they were minus several players this morning. Emily cleared her throat. "I don't know if he's coming, but I invited Pastor Speers to join us."

Both men turned skeptical expressions to her. "Think he can play?"

Honestly? No, though it would be disloyal to say so. Noah was the consummate urbanite. He dressed well, spoke well, played piano well, but the thought of him actually breaking a sweat? Not likely. Her handsome friend seemed more suited to elegant endeavors. Like yachting.

She lifted her shoulders. "I'm not sure. Like I said, I don't even know if he's planning to come."

The men shared a look before Trey spoke. "He's better than nothing. I'd hate to forfeit the game to the Titans. It's bad enough they always beat us, but to let them win without a fight . . ."

Sam turned to her. "Do you mind texting him again? Tell him we really need him."

"Sure." What did it say about her success in emotionally distancing herself from Noah when she was thrilled to have an excuse to contact him? She pulled out her phone and scrolled to his name. *Looks like the team is shorthanded. We could use your help. Can you make it?*

Almost immediately, dots appeared on the screen. *Parking now.*

Stepping away from the team for an unobstructed view, she looked toward Main Street. Sunlight flashed off his Tesla as Noah crossed behind it and stepped onto the sidewalk. He entered the park through the same gate she had and walked in the direction of the baseball diamond. As he grew closer, she waved. He lifted a hand in greeting and picked up his pace.

Several things went through her mind as he approached. Number one, Noah Speers was a perfect male specimen. Every time she saw him, it hit her like a new revelation. Head to toe, the man was magnificent.

Number two, inviting him had been an epic mistake.

He was close enough now she could make out the details of the clothes he wore. A neatly buttoned, white oxford shirt tucked into chino shorts in a rosy shade of pink, both starched and pressed to crispy perfection. Full-on preppy yachtsman.

As far as she could tell, the only concession he'd made to the coming game was wearing a pair of sneakers. New sneakers.

She didn't know if it was a case of his not being familiar with recreational attire, or that he hadn't brought any appropriate garments with him. Both scenarios were possibilities.

She cast a quick glance over her shoulder at the ragtag team, dressed in baggy gym shorts and T-shirts in varying stages of deterioration. Village Green did not do preppy.

They were going to eat him alive.

He stopped directly in front of her, eyes hidden behind mirrored sunglasses, and gave her one of his high-powered smiles. "Hey, Doc."

Her heart fluttered, another sure sign she wasn't winning the war in redirecting her affections. "Hi, Noah. Thanks for coming."

"Are you kidding?" He looked past her toward the gathered team. "I wouldn't miss an opportunity to hang with the handful of citizens who aren't collecting Social Security."

"Heh, heh." She gave him a weak laugh before shifting so her back was to the others. She lowered her voice. "The thing is, I think they take their softball really seriously."

He shrugged off her remark. "Not surprised. I've seen the town. A couple of hours of running bases on the weekend is probably the best they can hope for."

"Yes, well, what I'm trying to say—"

"Well, hey there, Pastor Speers." Trey joined them and extended his hand.

Noah accepted it. "Call me Noah. I remember you from church. It's Trey, right?"

"Good memory." He sized up the other man. "You ready for some ball?"

A long, shrill wolf whistle sounded from somewhere behind them. Sam appeared at Trey's side, giving Noah an exaggerated once-over. "Wow, Hotshot. You sure do look purty." He inhaled deeply. "Smell fancy too."

Emily wanted to die. When she'd invited him today, she'd hoped he'd get a little dose of small-town life, not a radical infusion of redneck testosterone. She took a step in Noah's direction, thinking to position herself between him and the threat. He placed a casual hand on her shoulder, applying just enough pressure to stop her.

His movie-star smile never faltered as he flicked a dismissive glance at his clothes. "What? These old things?"

Trey snorted a startled laugh.

Sam wasn't through. "You're mighty dressed up for a game of softball."

Another downward glance. "Just trying to show you boys the way."

"And where's your hat? You're gonna want something to keep the sun out of your eyes."

Noah screwed up his face in mock distress as he lifted his free hand to his head. "And risk messing up my hair? No way."

Emily pulled free of Noah's restraining hand and stepped into the middle to break it up when suddenly, inexplicably, all three men broke into raucous laughter. Huh? One minute they're sniping at one another, the next they're clapping one another on the back like it was all a joke?

She shook her head. With two younger brothers, she ought to be familiar with the incomprehensibility of male posturing.

Noah acquitted himself nicely. His use of humor to diffuse the testosterone-fueled moments and earn the respect of the locals was masterful.

But that was only round one.

It would take more than a quick mind to maintain his accepted status. If, as she feared, he was as hopeless at softball as he had been at the charcoal grill, he'd be a laughingstock by game's end.

This was not her problem. Whether or not he could hold up his head in Village Green would matter little, as he'd be gone in a week.

But it mattered to her.

Partly because he was here by her invitation, and she had some responsibility for him, but mostly because she just really liked him. And because she did, it was up to her to protect him.

"Speers, you've got right field."

Noah nodded his acceptance to Trey, who stood in the center of the circled team, handing out assignments. Right field in slow pitch rarely saw any action. They stuck the overdressed new guy where he could do the least damage.

Emily's arm shot up. "I'll take center field."

Trey frowned. "I thought I'd put you—"

"I'd like center field."

Noah lifted his brows. Based on the urgency in her voice, the doc must *really* like center field.

"Okay, Emily, you're in center field." Trey erased something on his clipboard, penciled in something else. "Jason, left field."

As Trey continued to assign positions, Emily edged closer to Noah and whispered, "We'll be next to each other."

"Apparently so."

"We can help each other out." Her wide-eyed expression and exaggerated nod told him there was more to this than outfield preference.

Ah. Now it made sense. Emily was shy around crowds; she'd told him so when they'd first met. Maybe standing next to him in the game, like she had at the covered-dish lunch, would put her at ease.

The fact she'd reached out to him in her need pleased him. He gave her a smile. "Good idea. I'll be happy to have you there."

She looked up at him from under the pink brim of her hat, her eyes full of secret, shared understanding. They were in this together.

Once the assignments were made, the team moved to take their positions. He and Emily stopped to pick up gloves from a stack of loaners before trotting across the packed dirt to the outfield.

"You'll want to stand over there." Emily stopped in center field and pointed to her right.

He frowned. For a second, it sounded like she didn't think he knew where to go. "Yeah, okay." Maybe she worried he'd get too far away.

She followed his progress, giving him an encouraging thumbs-up when he made it to his grassy post.

At nine thirty, the temperature was already in the high eighties. Not a cloud in the sky or the slightest hint of a breeze. The beautiful old trees scattered around the park were too far to offer cool shade. The sun blazed behind him, scorching his dress-shirt-covered back and uncovered head. Even with the sunscreen Emily'd provided and insisted he apply, he'd be fried by game's end.

No help for it. He hadn't packed any workout clothes for what was supposed to be an abbreviated stay. And though he'd found out about the game last evening, there was no place to shop for a T-shirt or ball cap. By seven o'clock, the entire town had closed down— rolled up the sidewalks for the night. One more mark against this blighted end of civilization.

He didn't know how the doctor stood it.

He glanced in her direction. With her attention on the soon-to-start game, she leaned slightly forward, hands propped on her knees. At least she'd dressed the part, with her navy, mid-thigh shorts and white, sleeveless T-shirt. Today she wore her dark hair in a long, thick braid threaded through the back of a bubblegum-pink ball cap. She looked fresh and feminine.

His gaze lingered. She was really very pretty. Not his type, of course, but if his taste ran to short, curvy women, Emily Cutler would be at the top of his list.

The crack of bat on ball drew his attention to the infield. The first batter had a solid hit and made it to base. Noah could hear the chatter as both teams reacted to the play.

A succession of strong batters put the opposing team up 2-0. The only activity in right field was a couple of bees buzzing around a clump of white clover.

"Left-handed batter," Emily called to him.

He sent her a thumbs-up, the warning giving him an excuse to look at her. Not that he hadn't been stealing glances all along. The doctor was a pleasure to watch.

While he combated boredom by studying her or the surrounding park, she focused one hundred percent on the game. As each batter came to the plate, she'd assume a ready position, bouncing lightly on the balls of her feet while waiting for the outcome of the swing. Once the play was over, she'd straighten, punch her fist into her glove, and call out encouragement to the team.

This athleticism was an appealing new dimension to the woman he'd previously admired for her brains and capacity for stillness. Had he thought she was short? Wrong. Emily was perfectly proportioned and moved with an unconscious grace—

Crack.

Whoa, fast-moving, shoulder-high ball coming his way.

Because he'd watched his teammate and not the game, he missed the swing. In the time it took to react to the incoming missile, Emily darted over, stretched out one of the shapely arms he'd been admiring, snatched the ball out of the air, and winged it to the second baseman for a neat out.

His one big chance for some action, and he blew it.

Inning over, they jogged side by side toward home plate. He gestured over his shoulder. "That was a beautiful play. Sorry I didn't hold up my end."

Instead of being justifiably miffed with his poor performance, she accepted his apology with a look of gentle understanding—the kind of automatic forgiveness people extended to an acknowledged goofus. Comprehension brought heat to his face.

She thought he was a loser.

When Trey and the cop were giving him a hard time, she'd been standing at his side. She probably assumed, as they did, that an over-dressed, city-boy preacher didn't have game. His thoughts fell into place like a line of toppling dominos. She hadn't insisted on center field because she was shy and needed him for moral support. She was there to cover for him.

Talk about humiliating. Worst part—that's exactly what happened.

He didn't care what the others thought about him, but no way he'd let her believe he was a loser.

They gathered with the others behind the rusty backstop. The sun beat down on them as Trey went over the batting lineup while the opposing team took the field. No surprise, Noah was dead last. After his lackluster job in the outfield, he was eager to redeem himself. He grabbed a bottle of water from the ice chest, then took his place at the far end of the bleacher, elbows on his knees and chin sunk into his hands, to wait his turn.

"You do know if you see a ball coming your way, you're supposed to swing at it," the cop taunted.

Noah didn't bother to look at him. "Thanks for the tip."

The opposing pitcher was a beast with a short, thick neck, wide barrel chest, and muscular arms with tattoos so dense it took Noah several minutes to realize the guy wore a tank top, not long sleeves. He powered the underhand pitches over the plate with such force and skill that Village Green had three outs before Noah had a turn at bat.

"It's okay, guys. It's still early." Trey rallied the team as they stood to retake their positions in the field. "We've got this."

Emily waited for Noah, and they walked out side by side in the sweltering heat. "I think we're in trouble. These guys are good. Where do you suppose they found that pitcher?"

He took another look over his shoulder at the hulk. "My guess? Biker bar. He's probably the bouncer." He smiled down at her. "Hey, nice hit, by the way."

"Thank you." The expression on her face said she'd have liked to have had something nice to say back to him. Unfortunately, he hadn't done anything worth complimenting.

At least when she stopped in center field and he continued past her to his post, she didn't coach him on where to stand.

She waved once he arrived at his now-trampled clump of clover. "Don't forget to keep an eye out for left-handed batters."

"Yeah." Lifting his hand in acknowledgment, he gave her a weak smile. "Thanks." *Sheesh.*

The Bikers—he'd forgotten their official team name—scored another run at the top of the second. They finished their at-bat without sending a single ball into right field. Noah refused to accept that he would go down as the biggest loser in Village Green softball history.

Bottom of the second, he got his first turn at bat.

Trey handed him a batting helmet. "Good luck, man."

"Thanks." Helmet in place, Noah picked up a bat and gave it a few practice swings on his way to home plate.

"Well, hey there, Cupcake." The pitcher smirked. "Where'd you get the fancy pink pants?"

There were times when it stunk to be a preacher. Not that he'd rush the mound and stuff the inked giant. For one thing, the guy had a hundred pounds on him. And then there was the whole poor-sportsmanship thing. But honestly, it'd be so gratifying to let fly a snarky comeback.

Not going to happen. As a believer committed to walking in a manner worthy of his calling, his only option was to grin and bear it.

Support came from an unexpected source. The cop, who'd hassled him since he'd arrived, stepped up behind the backstop. "Hang in there, man. Sometimes the whole *turn the other cheek* thing can be problematic, but you've got this."

"Thanks, bro." Noah turned to the pitcher. "Why don't you just throw the ball? We can compare tailoring later."

God was merciful, and Noah got a hit. Unfortunately, he grounded to the left and while he made it to first, his teammate on second got tagged. Three outs. Back to the field.

By the bottom of the last inning, the Bikers were up 5-2. Village Green had one more turn at bat. Noah got to the plate with two outs, bases loaded.

Everything was riding on him.

No pressure.

Sometime during the last inning, sweat stopped trickling down his face and back. Now, it poured. Perspiration mixed with sunscreen stung his eyes. His shirt was soaked.

As he pulled off his sunglasses to scrub his sleeve across his face, he visualized David standing before Goliath. Admittedly, his cause wasn't as righteous, but the similarities were unmistakable. An underdog before a jeering opponent.

His teammates on the bases called encouragement, as did those on the bench.

"You've got this, man." Trey handed him a helmet.

"'The Lord who delivered me from the paw of the lion and from the paw of the bear, He will deliver me from the hand of this Philistine.'"

Trey wrinkled his forehead. "Huh?"

Noah grinned as he reached for the bat. "That's Bible talk for 'I've got this, man.'"

The pitcher's mouth stretched into a smile. "Welcome back, Cupcake. You gonna get the final out so we can go home?"

Just as David must have considered the stones in his pouch before loading one into his sling, Noah considered his strategy. The only way Village Green wouldn't go down in ignominious defeat would be if he belted the ball hard enough and far enough that he and the people currently waiting on bases could get home.

All or nothing.

Silence fell as he gripped the bat and lifted it into position. No longer smiling, the pitcher slung the softball with such force it whistled through the air as it sailed past Noah.

"Strike one."

The calls from his team grew louder, Emily's above the rest. "Come on, Noah. Show him what you've got."

Help me, Lord.

Noah connected solidly with the next pitch, driving it into foul territory. The third baseman snagged it on the first bounce and tossed it to the mound.

"Strike two."

His nerves sparked as the tension built. He rolled his shoulders, scuffed his feet in the dirt.

All or nothing.

Instead of throwing the ball to Noah, the pitcher suddenly pivoted and shot the ball to third, a warning to the cop who was leading several paces from the base.

"Keep focused," Trey called. "Don't let him ice you."

Noah imagined the Philistine tried to ice David too—tried to distract him, get him off balance. Like the young shepherd, Noah wouldn't fall for it. He was one hundred percent in the game.

Perspiration rolled from his hairline into his eyes. His shirt clung to his back and arms as he lifted the bat to his shoulder.

Help me, Lord.

The pitch came low and fast. Eye on the ball, Noah swung with all his might. The solid *thunk* said the hit was good.

He dropped the bat and ran for first as though the Philistine army were on his heels. Vaguely aware of cheers, he touched his foot to the bag as he rounded for second.

The cheering intensified as runners crossed home plate. A quick tap on the corner of the base, and Noah sped for third.

"Hurry, Noah. Hurry."

Activity from the opposing team seemed to indicate they'd recovered the ball and were moving it infield. Time was running out.

"Come on, Noah." He recognized Emily's voice. "You can do it."

His feet flew down the baseline. Touched third. Raced for home.

"Come on, Preacher."

Now he heard the frenzied chatter from the Bikers. "Throw it home. Throw it home."

It was going to be close. Noah dug deep for a final burst of speed. At the last possible second, he dropped into a slide.

"Safe!"

CHAPTER EIGHT

"He made it!" Emily's disbelieving exclamation was half laugh, half cry. She clapped a hand over her thundering heart. The hold-your-breath tension of the last minutes uncoiled into a massive sigh of relief.

It wasn't pretty, but Noah's daring, last-minute slide managed to beat the ball to home plate by milliseconds. He was safe. They'd won the game.

The team surged to their feet, cheering and pumping their fists. She hung back, watching as they crowded around Noah—congratulating him and slapping him on the back. His face glowed with pleasure.

Her heart swelled with pride.

Trey herded the celebrants back to the bench so they could finish the inning. The next batter popped up the ball for a quick catch, and the game was officially over. Village Green, 6-5.

As the opposing team came off the field, they stopped by the home bleacher to offer their congratulations. The pitcher walked over just as Sam turned to Noah and said, "Well, Preacher, it looks like you've been hiding your light under a bushel."

The much-tattooed player froze, a look of dismay on his face. He stared at Noah. "You're a preacher? For real?"

Noah nodded.

The pitcher narrowed his eyes. "You don't look like a preacher."

Noah grinned. "I get that a lot."

After a long stretch of silence, the larger man extended a beefy hand toward him. "I'm sorry. I didn't mean to disrespect you."

Noah smiled warmly as he shook his hand. "I didn't take offense. What's a ball game without a little trash talk?"

His grace-filled response seemed to put the remorseful hulk at ease. "Thanks, man. Good game."

It took another half hour for congratulations and packing gear before the team finally headed across the grass toward their cars. Emily swung the strap of her bag over her shoulder and fell into step beside Noah.

"There you are." He smiled down at her, his eyes hidden behind mirrored lenses. "I thought you were avoiding me."

She hadn't expected him to notice her absence. "Not at all. Just giving you time with your fans."

He tipped back his head and laughed. "Talk about a reversal of fortunes. I was about to go down as the team washout, and instead I'm the guy everybody wants to buy lunch."

His humor was infectious, and a smile pulled at her lips. "It *was* an amazing hit."

Another rich laugh. "What you mean is, it was a miracle. Don't worry. I'm not offended. I admit, I did a whole lot of praying while standing at the plate. There was definitely an element of the miraculous involved."

Just then she happened to notice the back of his once-pristine sleeve. The rolled white cuff was caked with dirt and blood. "Oh, Noah. What have you done to your arm?"

He paused, twisting his elbow toward his face in an awkward attempt to see what she was talking about. "I must have scraped it when I slid into home."

"It's a mess. Come by my place, and we'll clean it up."

He shook his head. "Nope. I have a firm policy against visiting single women in their apartments." He tilted his face toward her. "Especially the pretty ones."

Pretty. Her heart fluttered with pleasure. Not kind or smart or hard-working. *Pretty.*

She blinked to reset her thoughts. "My apartment doesn't count. I'm a doctor."

He frowned as though she'd missed the point. "A *female* doctor."

Clearly, he wasn't budging. And the arm needed attention. The scrape didn't look serious, just dirty. "Then come by the clinic. Really, Noah. Let's get you cleaned up. I insist."

They exited the park through the iron gate onto the sun-drenched sidewalk on Main Street.

He turned left and pointed to his car at the curb. "Fine. I'll drive."

She looked at the expensive silver sedan and shook her head. "No way I'm sitting on those white seats. I'm filthy."

Ignoring her, he pulled open the passenger door. "Come on, Doc. It's too hot to ask a wounded man to walk. Get in. I insist."

He had a point. It *was* hot, and air-conditioning sounded amazing. Pulling off her ball cap, she climbed in and angled a vent toward her face. One perk of a luxury car must be its ability to cool off quickly, even after baking in the blistering sun.

In a minute, they pulled up in front of the clinic. A rush of cool air greeted them as she unlocked the glass door, turned on the lights, and ushered him inside.

She relocked the door behind them. "We'll use exam room one."

Her sneakers squeaked on the tile as she led the way through the waiting room and past the door separating the public and medical spaces. "Right in here."

After flipping on the overhead light, she stepped over to the sink to scrub her hands thoroughly. "Now, turn around, and let's see what we're dealing with."

Rather than sitting on the exam table, Noah stood at the foot, obediently angling his back to give her a better view of his arm. The scrape, running from elbow to wrist, was packed with debris, but shallow. The sluggish bleeding had stopped.

"The good news is, you won't need stitches." She delivered her diagnosis over his shoulder. "The bad news is, it looks like your clothes took the brunt of the slide. It is my considered medical opinion the shirt can be salvaged with a generous dose of bleach, but I'm not sure the shorts will recover."

"DOA, huh?" He chuckled. "No loss. They were a gift from my mom. I'm not a big fan of pink, so I had them in my trunk to return to the store. Providential, all things considered."

She glanced back at his garments. "The dirt marks give me a good idea of where you hit the hardest. Go ahead and remove your shirt. I want to check to be sure you didn't scrape up your side as well."

"It's nothing. Really."

"I'll be the judge of that. Take off your shirt."

His back to her, he shot her an unreadable look before pulling his shirt tails from his shorts, lifting the fabric, and exposing his torso.

She skimmed a fingertip along the edge of the abraded flesh below his ribcage.

Noah jumped as if electrified. "Hey, watch it. Your hands are cold."

Rattled, whether by his reaction or his bare skin, Emily cleared her throat. "The area is irritated, like a mild road rash. I think it will heal better left uncovered."

"Good." He went to work shoving the shirt back into his waistband.

She put out a hand to stop him. "Wait. What about your hip?"

He turned, lowering his head to look directly into her eyes. "If you think I'm going to drop my shorts for you, you're wrong."

Something about the combination of his proximity and silky tone caused her face to heat. "You don't have to drop them completely. Just lower them a little so I can see your hip."

"No. Way."

She pressed her lips together. "Noah, I'm a doctor."

"I don't care if you're the surgeon general. I'm keeping my pants on."

Maybe a different tack. "I admire your modesty, but there's no reason to be shy."

"I admire your tenacity, but the shorts stay."

They were eye to eye in the tiny exam room, his face inches from hers. She could see the darker rim around his golden-brown irises and feel the warmth of his breath. She sighed, a faint longing-filled hum.

"What?" he whispered.

What indeed? She was supposed to be *getting* over him, not *drooling* over him.

"I . . . uh—" Her gaze drifted to the top of his head as she searched for a response. A halo of tawny whorls replaced his usual ruthlessly tidy style. She lowered her eyes to his. "How did I not know you have curly hair?"

Scowling, he straightened, creating space between them, and the moment was gone. "Probably because I've made it my life's work to camouflage it."

Now that she'd noticed the curls, she couldn't look away. Instead of tight ringlets, each lock was a half-circle, ending in a spiky point. "Don't you like curls?"

He combed his fingers through the unruly strands. "They are the bane of my existence."

"But they're so pretty."

He met her eyes and frowned. "Exactly."

He looked so disgruntled, she laughed. Here she was, thrilled over the idea of being pretty, and this beautiful man was horrified by it. "I guess we're never satisfied with what we have. I've always wanted curls, and my hair is as straight as a paintbrush."

Once more he leaned in. "Your hair is beautiful." His gaze traveled slowly from the braid hanging over her shoulder to her face. "Looks like you got some sun on your nose."

She felt herself sliding back under his spell. "You too." Her voice was barely a whisper.

He smiled into her eyes. "I guess that's what happens when you stand out in the blazing sun for hours."

"I'm sorry you didn't have a hat."

"I tried to pick one up last night after you texted, but everything was closed."

She didn't know why they were speaking in hushed tones, but it imbued their unremarkable conversation with an exciting sense of intimacy. "I'm so sorry, Noah. I never considered you wouldn't have access to workout clothes when I invited you."

"You and everybody else. You heard the catcalls. The locals think I'm an ignorant city boy who doesn't know how to dress appropriately."

The memory of her own disloyal thoughts about a yuppie yachtsman caused her to grimace. "Why didn't you explain? You should have defended yourself."

He lifted his shoulders dismissively. "Didn't see the point. I'll be gone in a few days."

"But I don't want them to think you're clueless."

The corners of his mouth turned up. "Doc, I've been in the public eye my whole life. Early on, I learned you can't please everyone. So, I don't try. I only care about the opinions of the people who truly matter to me." His gaze locked with hers. "I'm including you in that group."

"Thank you. That means a lot."

His eyes lit. "Which doesn't mean I'm dropping my shorts."

The humor yanked her back from her dreamy reverie. She laughed. "So you keep saying. Come on, Preacher. Let's get you cleaned up."

She turned on the faucet and adjusted the temperature of the water, then waved him over. "Put your arm under the spray."

The small exam room shrank further as all six-plus feet of him slid in beside her. He held his arm under the warm flow.

The only way to access the cut was by pressing in close, her shoulder resting against his side. She poured liquid cleanser on the wound, then let the gentle spray slough over it. Bits of dirt and grass ran into the sink. When, at last, the water ran clear and no dirt remained, she turned off the faucet. Following another inspection, she carefully blotted the area with a lint-free cloth.

"Watch your head." After he stepped back, she reached up and opened the cabinet above them. "I'm going to apply an antibiotic ointment, then cover it with a bandage to keep out bacteria. You'll need to keep the dressing dry—"

He shook his head. "That's going to be a problem. As soon as I walk out of here, I'm going back to Dale's to take the world's longest shower. I stink."

"You don't stink." And she was close enough to know. He

smelled delicious, not that she would embarrass either of them by saying so. "You smell healthy—like hot sun and exertion. Trust me. With two brothers, I know stink."

"If you say so." He glanced around. "Are we done?"

"Almost." She pulled several boxes from the cabinet and set them on the counter by the sink. "Let me get some bandages and ointment for you to use after your shower. Apply the cream to the affected area and cover it with a fresh dressing every day. Dale will have to help you, since it's your right arm." She gave him a stern look. "I want you to keep an eye out for infection."

He nodded with sham solemnity. "Yes, Doctor."

"And if you skinned your hip—"

"—you'll be the last person to know."

They shared a laugh.

She assembled a dozen medical dressings, several rolls of tape, and a handful of sample packets of antibacterial cream, and placed them in a small plastic bag one of the pharmaceutical reps had left behind. She handed it to him before replacing the boxes overhead. "Let me know if you need more."

"I could wrap myself like a mummy with what you've given me. Come on, Doc. Let's go."

They retraced their steps to the front door, switching off lights along the way. Emily locked up and dropped the keys in her handbag. She glanced at his car, then back at him. "Why don't you head to Dale's and get your shower? I live close by. I'll walk."

"I thought you said I didn't stink."

"You don't. I know you're eager to get cleaned—"

His grin said he enjoyed teasing her. He opened the passenger door. "Get in the car. There's no way I'm leaving you out here to melt."

Because it would give her a few more minutes with him, she

agreed without protest. She directed him the short distance from her clinic to the narrow parking lot behind her apartment. "This is my stop."

He glanced at the building and frowned. "You live in an abandoned store?"

She laughed as she pointed to the second story. "My apartment is up there. It's beautiful."

"I'll have to take your word for it."

Joy welled inside her. He'd have to take her word for it because he wouldn't be visiting. And he wouldn't be visiting because he didn't visit the apartments of single, pretty women. And he thought she was pretty.

Energized despite the heat, she gathered her bag and cap, swung open the door, and climbed out of the car. Hand on the window, she leaned down to smile at him. "Thank you for the ride."

He nodded. "My pleasure. Thanks for patching me up."

"My pleasure." She continued to stand there, smiling at him. *Okay, Emily, that's enough. Let the man go.* She straightened and stepped back from the car. "Well, goodbye."

She'd taken two steps toward the apartment entrance when he called after her, "Hey, are you planning to join the team for lunch at Estelle's?"

She turned back, ridiculously pleased to continue their conversation. "I thought I might. How about you?"

"Absolutely. I told you they were fighting over who could buy me lunch."

She folded her arms across her chest and sent him a look of mock indignation. "I scored a run, and nobody offered to buy mine."

He shook his head as though distressed. "That's just not right. Tell you what. I'll pay for yours."

She waved away his offer. "Oh, no, I was just kidding."

"Sorry. No take backs. If you get to the restaurant before me, do me a favor and save me a seat."

She bobbed her head. "Okay. Sure."

"See you in a bit."

Noah was late. He'd stayed in the shower until he'd used every last drop of hot water. The spray stung the scrape on his arm and the raspberry that stretched from the bottom of his ribs to his lower thigh, but he didn't care. It felt so amazing to be clean.

He parked between two pickup trucks about a block from Estelle's and shut off the engine. Sunlight beat down on his head as he loped along the sidewalk and ducked into the diner.

The owner met him at the door, an empty tray under her arm. She smiled at him over the top of her half-glasses. "Hey, Pastor Speers. The team's over there by the window."

With her free hand, she pointed through the crowd toward a long table composed of several smaller tables pushed together. "Have a seat, and I'll be by to get your order in a minute. What are you drinking?"

"Sweet tea, please." He'd already guzzled a quart of water and was still parched. "The biggest glass you've got."

She grinned. "Softball is hot work this time of year. By the way, congratulations."

News must travel fast in small towns. "Thank you."

The restaurant drew a big Saturday crowd. Country music blended with the lively buzz of conversation as he wove through the occupied tables toward the team.

"Here he is!" Trey sounded as though they'd been waiting for him to arrive. "Come, sit down."

Noah lifted his hand in greeting before making his way around to the empty chair between Emily and the cop.

"Look at you. All gussied up again." Sam's face looked pained. "Don't you own a T-shirt or a pair of jeans?"

"Hush, Sam." His wife, Riley, smacked his arm. "Emily just explained."

After a quick downward glance at his polo shirt and khakis, Noah looked from Riley to Emily. "Explained what?"

Sam cocked a thumb at Emily. "Your friend here just reamed us out for messing with you about your clothes. She said you didn't anticipate a softball game when you packed."

Emily looked up at Noah, her blue eyes filled with amused exasperation. "I did *not* ream them out."

"Why didn't you tell us?" Eden asked. "We could have scrounged up something for you to wear." She pointed to her husband. "You and Joe are about the same size."

He lowered into his chair, careful not to jostle his stiffening wound. "Thanks for the offer. If I find myself drafted for another game before I leave, I'll take you up on it."

"That was quite a hit," Trey said. "I'm guessing that wasn't your first time to play."

Noah shook his head. "I played intramural sports in college."

"Where'd you go to school?"

"Baylor."

Estelle arrived and set a tall red plastic glass of iced tea in front of him before looking around the table. "Everybody ready to order?"

The cop pointed to Noah. "Start with the preacher, and put his tab on mine, would you, Estelle?"

"Thanks, man." Noah turned and smiled at the owner. "I'll have a burger, medium, with everything, and a side of fries. And keep the sweet tea coming."

Emily ordered after him. When Estelle moved on to Eden, Noah leaned toward Emily. The doctor smelled fresh, her long hair still damp. "Thanks for saving a seat for me," he whispered.

"Happy to do it," she whispered back. "Feel better?"

"Like a new man. That's why I was late. I couldn't make myself get out of the shower."

Smiling, she nodded. "I know what you mean. Clean never felt so good." She repositioned in her chair to face him and held out a hand. "Let me see your arm."

He extended the bandaged appendage for her inspection. "Dale did a nice job."

Her slender fingers were cool on his wrist and upper arm as she studied it. "Yes, he did. I know who to call if I need a backup medical assistant."

By now their end of the table had finished ordering and turned their attention to Emily and him.

"Did you hurt yourself?" Eden asked.

He lowered his arm to his side, away from curious stares. "Not really. Just a little scrape."

Joe looked at him with respect. "Pretty bold move to slide like that."

Noah shrugged. "Pure desperation. I could tell they were closing in. I didn't know how much time I had left. We were so close . . ." *And I couldn't let the game end with the doctor thinking I'm a loser.*

"I'm glad you did it." Trey's wife, Hallie, lifted a hand to qualify her statement. "I'm not glad you were hurt, of course, but I am so sick of them beating us."

Trey lowered his glass and nodded. "We haven't won against them in years."

"And every time they beat us, they gloat." Hallie exhaled loudly as she rolled her eyes. "I don't have to tell you how obnoxious they are."

Noah grinned. "The cupcake thing was wearing thin."

"Amen," Emily mumbled under her breath.

"At least you got your revenge." Hallie grinned. "Did you see the pitcher's face when he realized he'd insulted a preacher? He looked so horrified. I half expected him to burst into tears."

Noah chuckled. "Now, *that* would be a sight worth seeing."

They all laughed and just that quickly, the atmosphere shifted. Instead of polite acquaintances struggling to find common ground with a stranger, Noah was one of them.

As everyone talked, sometimes over one another, he pieced together who was who. Trey, Sam the cop, and Joe were locals— childhood friends born and raised in Village Green. Despite that, he discovered he liked all three men. Each was educated and well spoken. All appeared to be active in the community and, from the looks of things, happily married.

From listening to the conversations, he learned their wives, also friends, were relatively new to town. Hallie, Trey's wife, had been born in Village Green but left right after high school. Ten years later, when she returned to town to care for her mother, she'd reconnected with Trey, her high school sweetheart.

Eden was married to Joe, the quiet guy. Emily whispered they were her landlords, as well as owners of the bakery she'd told him about. Apparently, Eden and her young son had recently relocated to Village Green from Florida.

The newest arrival, and to his thinking the most interesting story, was Riley, the cop's wife. The schoolteacher had moved from Oklahoma to escape a stalker. Somehow the guy had tracked her here, and she and Sam had apprehended him and packed him off to prison. *Cool.*

Though the women couldn't have known one another for more than a year, they appeared to be genuinely close. A man experienced in reading people, Noah didn't pick up on any of the underlying competitiveness or animosity that frequently accompanied a female gathering of any size.

The other members of the team, Darcie and Jason and a guy whose name he couldn't remember, were there with their families. They sat far enough down the extended rectangular table that they had their own conversation going.

It took several trips for Estelle to bring all the food. When the last plate was delivered, and drinks refilled, Trey asked Noah to say grace.

"Sure." He bowed his head, centering his thoughts on the Source of every good thing. "Mighty One, we bless You. We thank You for our victory, delicious food, and friends to share it with. Help us to glorify You. In Jesus's name. Amen."

For several minutes, talk ceased as everyone dug into their meals. His hamburger was delicious—perfectly seasoned and grilled.

Between bites, he leaned toward Emily. "How's your burger?"

Her mouth full, she nodded enthusiastically. Once she'd swallowed, she asked, "How's yours?"

"Best I've ever had. And I don't think that's entirely postgame starvation talking."

She lowered her half-eaten sandwich to stare at him in mock disbelief. "Are you saying something about this *backwater burg* measures up to your exacting, big-city standards?"

He grinned. "Maybe. But if you tell anyone, I'll deny it."

Her blue eyes danced. "Your secret is safe with me."

Their near-whispered conversation caught the attention of the group. He could feel all eyes on them when Eden pointed first to him then Emily and asked, "So, how do you two know each other?"

He looked to Emily, who nodded to him to answer the question. "We met at Dale's when I came into town a week ago."

"Oh." Eden frowned. "For some reason, I thought you'd known each other longer. You seem, I don't know . . . friendly."

He shrugged. "No, just a week."

The conversation moved on to another topic, but Noah's thoughts stayed on the doctor. For no readily apparent reason, they *were* friendly for their short acquaintance. Other than their faith and a love of piano, they were basically so different, and yet, he felt a connection to her.

He liked her. He trusted her. He valued her insight.

She'd provided companionship and a listening ear in a lonely time.

He thought back to the surprising electricity sparking between them at the clinic. Didn't see that coming. The unexpected attraction had hit him in the gut.

What he wasn't going to do was allow himself to make more of their relationship than what was there. They were friends. Arguably, good friends. With a hefty dose of attraction thrown in. But soon he'd be gone, back to his real life and the calling God entrusted to him, and he'd never see her again.

He angled toward Emily as she answered a question. He enjoyed listening to her—both for her informed answers and the soothing timbre of her voice. As always, she spoke with a mixture of quiet confidence and humility.

As he looked at the women seated around the table today, all of whom were attractive, he realized the doctor fit right in. When they first met, he'd equated her simple dress and lack of cosmetics with unattractiveness. Compared to the women in his Houston circle, all lacquered and perfumed, Emily was plain.

How could he have been so blind?

Her long hair, like black silk, was pulled into the usual braid. More serviceable than stylish, the simple treatment suited the practical woman. Her unpainted smile was full and warm, her teeth straight and white without the artificial symmetry of those, like himself, who'd worn braces for years. And her blue eyes . . .

There was something very appealing about her natural kind of beauty.

She must have felt his gaze because she turned to him with a puzzled frown. "What?"

He shook his head. He wasn't ready to share his epiphany— that something about her challenged his long-held convictions about beauty. "Nothing."

The team lingered at the table after they'd eaten their fill and Estelle removed their plates. Noah listened as they shared stories about their lives. What struck him most was how each laugh or teasing remark was underscored with obvious affection. These people meant something to one another.

At last, Trey stood and addressed the group. "It's probably time to get out of here and let Estelle have the tables back. Thanks again, everyone, for a great game. We've got another one scheduled in two weeks. I'll text you with the details."

Noah turned to Sam. "Thanks for lunch."

The cop smiled. "No problem. It was the least I could do for the man who batted us to a win." His expression turned sly. "Of course, I had hoped you'd feel sufficiently in my debt that when I asked to borrow your sweet ride, you'd say yes."

His wife, who'd been listening over his shoulder, drilled her elbow into his side. "Sam!"

"What?" He shot her a look of innocence. "I've never ridden in a Tesla. It'd be so cool."

Noah laughed. "It's yours. Anytime."

He had the satisfaction of watching the cop's jaw drop. "No kidding?"

"Honest. Just let me know when. Let me give you my cell number. I'll be in town for another week."

Sam looked him square in the eye as he pulled his phone from his pocket. "I'm going to take you up on it."

"I hope you do." Noah clapped him on the back before turning to Emily. "You ready to go?"

She nodded.

He waved at the group lingering at the table. "We're out of here."

They walked out to a chorus of goodbyes.

Noah held open the restaurant door for Emily, and they stepped out into the oppressive afternoon heat. "Let me drive you home."

She hesitated as she slipped on her sunglasses. "It's hardly worth the trip. I live just around the corner."

"It's no trouble, and if your face feels like mine, you've had enough sun for the day."

She lifted a hand to her nose. "It does feel a bit burned. Okay." She smiled up at him. "That's nice."

Honestly, he didn't care about the heat or sun. He just wasn't quite ready for the afternoon to end. More specifically, he wasn't ready to say goodbye to her. He rounded the car and opened the passenger door before climbing in on his side and firing up the engine. After the initial blast of hot air, the vent poured out a solid stream of refreshing cold.

Emily tilted her head in the direction of the diner. "That was fun."

"I thought so too." He backed into the street before directing a look at her. "Don't I remember you telling me you're shy?"

Hands folded in her lap, she sent him a prim smile. "I believe my exact words were I'm introverted."

"Potayto, potahto."

That earned a chuckle. "As a rule, I'm very uncomfortable in gatherings like that, but something about the people here—"

"They're really friendly."

"True, but it's more than that. They've made me feel like family from the moment I pulled into town. I can't explain it, but I fit here." She offered him a baffled shrug.

A week ago, even yesterday, he'd have said he couldn't think of anything worse. That fitting into Village Green was like a death sentence. But sitting at the table over lunch, watching the team interact, he caught a glimpse of what she'd tried to articulate.

"They like you too." The earnest expression on Emily's face said his acceptance mattered to her. "I wasn't so sure when they were teasing you about your clothes."

"So, you set them all straight."

She sent him an apologetic frown before dropping her gaze to her hands. "I know you said you didn't need to explain, but I couldn't let them think less of you." She lifted her eyes to his. "I did not, however, ream them out."

He laughed. "Thank you for defending me."

She grinned. "I don't blame you for laughing at me, but I couldn't let it go. I hated for them to miss seeing the man I see."

No. Definitely not laughing at her. He reveled in the pure pleasure of having an incredible woman like her at his back.

He thought about her trying to insert her petite self between him and Trey and Sam when it appeared they weren't playing nice.

He didn't know what she thought she could do against the much larger opposition, but he'd been unbelievably touched she'd try.

Then she'd covered for his carelessness in the outfield. Finally, she finished off the day by taking on the entire team in defense of his wardrobe.

What man wouldn't be blessed to have such a powerful advocate in his corner?

"I'm not laughing at you. I'm laughing at my good fortune in finding a loyal friend like you."

When he pulled up outside the brown metal door leading into her apartment building, he considered asking her to come by the church tonight and play piano with him. It'd be fun to spend time together—just the two of them.

But it would also be unwise. He was leaving in a week.

Sighing, he shifted the car into park. "See you at church, Doc. Save me a seat."

CHAPTER NINE

Monday morning, Emily glanced up from her computer screen at the knock on her office door.

Jodi peered around the door. "Dr. Cutler, Hallie Gunther is here for her consultation."

"Thank you. Will you bring her back to my office, please?"

Emily had interned under a physician who'd conducted patient consults in his office rather than in an exam room. His rationale, that people think and respond more clearly in a comfortable, personal environment, had resonated with her. She'd decided that when she had her own practice and patients, she'd follow his example.

She slipped on her white coat and met Hallie at the door. "Good morning. Come in."

"Hi, Dr. Cutler." Hallie grimaced self-consciously. "That sounded weird."

"Agreed. Emily works for me." She pointed to the pair of chairs in front of her desk. "Please, sit down."

Hallie moved to the closest one, glancing around the room before lowering into the seat. "I like your office."

"Thank you." Emily surveyed the small space. "It's a work in progress. The furniture is hand-me-downs from the previous doctor. I want to fix the place up, but I've discovered I don't have a knack for decorating."

Hallie nodded emphatically. "Me, either. I have this fear of messing up, then being stuck forever with my bad choices."

Emily smiled at the perfect summation of her own fears. "Exactly."

"There's a woman in town, Mary Jo Piermont, who loves to decorate. You may have met her at church. She redoes her home all the time—it's like a hobby—and everything is always magazine-beautiful. If you like, I'll introduce you to her on Sunday. Maybe she could give you some pointers."

"That would be great. Any assistance would be appreciated." Instead of moving to her chair behind the desk, Emily propped against the corner and faced her friend. "Now, tell me what's going on with you."

Hallie's beaming smile said it all. "I'm pregnant."

Emily felt her insides go to mush. She loved babies. And new mothers with babies. And the glow of new mothers expecting babies. She clasped her hands over her heart. "Omigosh! Congratulations. That's so exciting."

Hallie bobbed her head, her shoulder-length brown hair swaying. "I just found out a week ago after I took one of those drug-store tests. I didn't play softball on Saturday because I've been spotting a little." She placed a protective hand over her abdomen. "I was worried I might hurt the baby."

Emily nodded. "Spotting in the first weeks is not uncommon. It happens as the egg imbeds in the uterine wall. Still, you'll want to talk with your doctor about it."

Hallie dropped her gaze to her hands folded in her lap. "That's why I'm here." She lifted a hopeful look to Emily. "I'd like you to be my doctor."

Hallie's confidence in her, that she would entrust the health of her baby to Emily, brought a warm flush of pleasure to her face. She sighed. "I'm so honored you asked me. But as much as I'd love to, I can't see maternity cases. The university medical group who set up this clinic considered the possibility of providing OB/GYN services but decided against it. Because Village Green is so small, with a predominantly older population, they felt they couldn't justify the expense of additional equipment."

Hallie's face fell. "I understand."

"There are several clinics in Corsicana. If you like, I can do a little digging and see if there's a particular doctor to recommend."

"Thank you." Disappointment shown around the edges of her half-smile. "I'd appreciate it."

Emily leaned toward her and smiled gently. "Even though I can't be your doctor, I want to hear everything. Let's start with how far along you are."

The opportunity to talk about her pregnancy brought the earlier radiance back to Hallie's face. "About six weeks." She held Emily's gaze. "We're not telling anyone yet."

Emily felt the honor and weight of being entrusted with her secret. She nodded. "I understand. How are you feeling?"

Another wide smile. "Good. Tired. I've suddenly become a nap person. I need an hour of sleep after lunch, or I can hardly function. The weirdest thing I've noticed is, I've developed a hypersensitive sense of smell, to the point where I hate to open the refrigerator." She put a hand over her mouth as if stifling a gag. "And don't get me started on raw meat."

Emily laughed. "All completely normal. And usually it'll pass after your first trimester. Does your husband cook?"

"Some. Trey likes to grill."

"You might recruit him to take over kitchen duty, at least until the sensitivity passes."

"That's a great idea." Hallie's eyes took on a mischievous gleam. "Can I tell him he *has* to cook? Doctor's orders?"

Emily nodded. "By all means. I'll send you with a prescription."

Their conspiratorial laughter further cemented the fledgling bond of friendship.

Hallie considered her for a moment. "Trey and I should have you and Noah over for dinner sometime."

Emily stilled, her hands braced on either side of her on the desk, her expression carefully neutral. "That would be nice."

Hallie frowned, eyes on Emily's face. "Did I say something wrong? I thought you two were together. You know, a couple."

Emily shook her head. "No. We're not together. Just friends."

Hallie narrowed her eyes. "Are you sure? Because from what I saw, it looked like more than friendship."

A mortifying thought crossed Emily's mind. What if her yet-to-be-extinguished crush on Noah showed in her actions? Was all of Village Green aware of her unrequited infatuation? She tried for a smile of supreme indifference. "No. Noah's a really great guy. But definitely out of my league."

Hallie sent her a puzzled frown. "Why would you say he's out of your league?"

Emily stared at her new friend in astonishment. "Have you *looked* at him?"

Hallie laughed. "Yes. And he's very good-looking. But then, so are you."

Emily pulled a pad of paper and pen from the pocket of her lab coat. She glanced at Hallie before making a note on the page. "While finding you an OB/GYN, I'm going to look for an eye doctor as well. It's obvious you need glasses."

Hallie laughed as she tapped the side of her face. "I wear

contacts. My corrected vision is twenty-twenty. You can believe me when I say you're lovely."

Emily's cheeks heated with pleasure. "Thank you." Because Hallie was a comfortable person to talk to, a safe place to confide, she lowered her eyes and shared her own precious secret. "Noah told me I'm pretty. Twice."

Hallie treated the whispered confidence with loyal gravity. "Nothing wrong with his eyesight."

Gaze trained on her hands folded in her lap, Emily confessed, "No one's ever told me that before. I get a lot of *brainy* and *big-hearted*, but never *pretty*. The weird thing is, knowing he sees me that way makes me want to be pretty."

"Makes perfect sense."

Emily felt the tension ease in her chest. It felt great, liberating even, to talk about her feelings with someone who understood. "I haven't put much effort into my appearance over the last few years. Medical school and residency were such a physical and emotional drain that showering every day was the pinnacle of my self-care aspirations."

Hallie laughed.

"Now that I've got the time and energy to expend on myself, I'm not sure where to start. It's kind of like decorating. I know I need an upgrade, but where to begin? All I know is, it's time to replace the dedicated-student look with something a bit more polished." She sent her friend a shy grin. "And pretty."

Hallie took a moment to study her. "Personally, I think you look amazing, but as a woman who knows the power of appearance, I believe it's wise to take a hard look at yourself occasionally and see where you can tweak things to get the image you want to project."

She paused, tapping a fingertip to her lips. "If you want to up your game, I think we should plan a day in Fort Worth."

Emily frowned. "What's in Fort Worth?"

"Everything." Hallie glanced toward the door before lowering her voice. "My husband is a card-carrying member of the chamber of commerce and therefore doesn't like me to admit it, but one of the realities of small-town life is the lack of decent shopping. And unless you want to get beauty advice at Biddie's Henhouse, we're going to have to go to the big city."

Emily snorted a laugh. "Biddie's Henhouse? Really?"

Hallie raised her right hand as if taking an oath. "Honest. Miss Biddie has a beauty shop in a shed her husband built behind her house. You have to walk around her vegetable garden to get to it. Biddie's been doing smelly spiral perms back there, Tuesday through Saturday by appointment only, since I was in elementary school. My mom's a huge fan."

A vision of the tightly curled blue-white hair she'd seen on plenty of heads around town came to mind. "Oh."

Hallie nodded. "Exactly. If you're serious about an upgrade, we need to go to Fort Worth."

"Okay, but I know you're busy." And sleepy. And queasy. "I feel bad asking you to go with me."

"Are you kidding? I love this kind of stuff." Hallie shot her a smile. "And besides, you didn't ask. I volunteered, remember? When you've known me longer, you'll realize I'm always up for an opportunity to shop. And I have a hair stylist there I love." She bent, pulled her phone from her bag she'd propped against the chair leg, and scanned the screen. "I'm looking at my calendar. What are you doing Saturday?"

Emily shrugged. "Nothing."

"Okay." She typed in something, then slipped her phone back into her bag. "I'll call and see if I can get you into the salon this weekend. If so, we'll make a day of it. Salon, lunch, and some serious shopping."

Emily felt like Cinderella faced with her fairy godmother. Help to find flattering clothes and a hairstyle that didn't make her look like a camp counselor? She clasped her palms together to keep from bursting into excited clapping. "That sounds great. Really. Thank you so much."

"My pleasure." Hallie glanced at her watch. "I didn't mean to take so much time. I need to let you get to your next patient." She gathered her purse and stood. "Once I know what's going on, I'll text you the details."

"Perfect." Emily walked her to the door. "And I'll get the scoop on a good OB/GYN in the area and send you the information. You and the baby will want to get started on prenatal care as soon as possible."

The mention of the baby brought a soft glow to Hallie's brown eyes. "Thank you." She paused on the threshold. "I'm sorry you won't be my doctor, but a shopping buddy is the next best thing." She walked into the hall, stopped, and turned back to whisper, "And upgrade or no, I think you and Noah make a beautiful couple."

Occupied with patients all morning, Emily didn't get out inquiries about an obstetrician for Hallie until noon. After she sent off the last email, she pulled her lunch from the bottom desk drawer and spread it out in front of her on a paper napkin. Carrot and celery sticks, two pickle spears, and a peanut butter and jelly sandwich on whole wheat bread. She took a bite of the sandwich and sighed with contentment.

God was so good. In her short tenure in Village Green, He'd provided her with a lovely home and office, and some truly wonderful friends.

As her gaze traveled the windowless room with its masculine

dark paneling, she thought about Hallie's offer to connect her with the woman from church who liked to decorate. Another blessing. The place obviously needed work, but she had no idea where to begin. She knew what she liked when she saw it, but visualizing changes—pulling ideas out of thin air—was beyond her scope of talent. Hopefully, Hallie's friend could offer some guidance.

Honestly, Hallie's offer to act as a shopping buddy and help her upgrade her own look excited her the most. Since meeting Noah, she realized she'd set her self-care benchmark too low. She wanted to be pretty but didn't know where to start. Fun and stylish Hallie would be the perfect guide.

Practical by nature, Emily couldn't see herself as one of those people who lived for fashion, but the idea of looking put-together held a wondrous appeal.

She'd never be as beautiful as Noah, but she could be the very best version of herself.

"You want me to do what?" Noah's voice ended in a not-so-manly squeak.

Dale stood beside him in the small kitchen, the sun angling through the glass door. The wood-look countertop was cluttered with bowls and knives, and bits of vegetable remnants were scattered across the cutting board. "Put your hands in there and mix all the ingredients together."

Noah screwed up his face. "That's what I thought you said." He regarded the blue bowl, heaped with raw hamburger and chopped vegetables, with misgiving. At some point, Dale had added a raw egg. Since he couldn't see it, it must have slid to the bottom.

He turned to his friend. "You're not messing with me, are you? I mean, I don't see why I can't use a spoon."

"I'm giving it to you straight." Dale's eyes danced with amusement as he delivered the news. "You can't get a good blend without using your fingers."

Noah heaved a sigh of resignation. He pushed his rolled sleeves past his elbows, took a deep breath, and plunged his hands into the cold, slippery mess. He looked over at his grinning mentor. "This is disgusting. You know that, right?"

Dale's grin widened. "It was your choice. You could have chopped vegetables instead."

"No, sir, not when I saw that monster onion waiting on the cutting board. I haven't fully recovered my eyesight from the last onion I faced."

Dale laughed.

Noah continued to squish the ingredients with his fingers while Dale looked on. "How hot does the oven have to be to cook out all the germs I've contributed to the mix by sticking my bare hands in here?"

"By the time it bakes for an hour, it'll be germ-free." He leaned around Noah to glance into the bowl. "Okay, that looks good. Go ahead and put it in the pan."

Noah scooped up the gloppy mixture and dropped it into the waiting metal container. He immediately crossed to the sink and held his hands under the hottest water he could tolerate. He soaped up, scrubbed vigorously, and rinsed, then repeated the procedure to remove the last bit of waxy residue. He nodded toward the finished product. "Does everybody make meat loaf like that? With their hands?"

"Never taken a poll on it, but I imagine so." Dale placed it in the oven and closed the door.

Noah grimaced. "No wonder I've never wanted to try it."

Dale gaped at him with wide-eyed incredulity. "You've never eaten meat loaf?"

"No, sir. Not once." He finished drying his hands on a paper towel. "Meat. Loaf. Just the name is off-putting."

Chuckling, Dale slapped him on the back. "Son, you're in for a real treat. My Betty used to fix this for us pretty regularly. When we were first married, she made it because it was economical. Our budget was so tight, meat was a real luxury. Thrifty homemakers add breadcrumbs and vegetables into the ground meat to stretch out the portions."

Who knew? Since Noah arrived in Village Green, not a single day passed that he didn't learn something from Dale. Beyond rudimentary cooking skills, he'd gained so many insights into life. Into himself.

Like budgeting, a word he'd only heard in passing. When he attended college and divinity school, he'd lived on a fixed amount of money, but it had been so generous, there was never a need to stretch it. He remembered hearing friends laugh about living on ramen noodles until they received their next deposit, but he'd never bothered to consider what that actually meant.

Noah frowned. How many opportunities to share grace and compassion had he missed because he'd been too caught up in his own life to care?

Something about this wise old man touched a previously unreached part of Noah. Their short acquaintance had already made an immeasurable impact on his life.

He smiled at his host. "Thank you for broadening my horizons."

Dale grinned. "Don't thank me until you taste it."

"The meat loaf is only a small part of what I'm grateful for."

The older man met his eyes and nodded with understanding. "Then, you're welcome."

Standing at the edge of the kitchen in a shaft of light filtering through the window, Noah had an epiphany. Since the day he arrived in town, he'd questioned what he was doing here. He knew God and His purposes are good, but this sidetrack didn't feel good. *Except meeting Emily, of course.* Suddenly, he saw His purpose in dragging him to Village Green wasn't to benefit this humble servant of God. On the contrary, the blessings were all Noah's.

Noah's mind continued to churn as he set the table for dinner, another useful skill he'd picked up during his stay. He remembered griping as he'd pulled into Dale's driveway, accusing the Almighty of making a mistake in sending him here.

If this was a test, he'd failed.

Instead of acting like a man of God, he'd responded to the unwanted trip like a spoiled child. He'd pulled into town with an attitude of superiority. As though he deserved better accommodations. Better treatment. He remembered his horror when Emily applied the term *celebrity* to him. He'd tried to deny it, but she'd spoken truth. Noah grimaced. At home, people treated him as a celebrity, and he'd come to expect it.

What happened? When had he developed a sense of entitlement? Where had he derailed from his calling to imitate his Savior?

Thoroughly sickened as well as repentant, he breathed a prayer as he placed the two plates across from each other at the little round table, asking God to forgive him for being a jerk. He thanked Him for bringing Dale into his life. He ended with the heartfelt request that he not miss any heaven-intended lessons before he returned to Houston.

An hour later, the men settled at the table. After asking the blessing, Dale watched expectantly while Noah took his first bite.

Mmm. Really tasty. Noah nodded as he chewed. "I admit it. Despite my insider's knowledge about the whole mix-it-with-your-hands thing, this meat loaf is delicious. I mean it. Seriously delicious. Kudos to Betty for an excellent recipe."

"Told you," Dale crowed with obvious delight.

Noah laughed at his smug expression. "I'm really going to miss you." The words were out of his mouth before he gave them much thought, but they were absolutely true. He *would* miss the old guy.

Dale smiled, his blue eyes warm. "And I, you. We make good roommates. Though I've thoroughly enjoyed your company, I know it will soon be time for you to get back to your responsibilities at home. I'm truly sorry I didn't have the opportunity to listen to you preach while you were here."

Noah felt the last piece of the puzzle slide into place. What if cooking skills, the ability to see beyond his own selfishness, even meeting Emily were only precursors to His real purpose? What if God dragged him here, to the end of the earth, to equip him to preach?

For years Noah had insisted he was ready to take the pulpit, but God had a different opinion. Maybe the endless, frustrating delays were to bring him to a place of humility and willingness to learn.

He'd always considered himself an excellent communicator. Compelling. Dynamic. Though he'd taken countless classes on sermon prep and delivery, his presentation closely mirrored that of his father and grandfather. Both men leaned heavily on the dramatic—exaggerated gestures and theatrical voice inflection. More oration than conversation. Tent-meeting style rather than talky. Because the approach caught and held the attention of the congregation, Noah followed suit. If it's not broke, don't fix it.

In contrast, Dale preached informally, almost like a friend sharing a discovery with another friend. It should have been boring, but it wasn't. If anything, his unembellished presentation seemed to focus the spotlight on the Word of God and not the speaker. He humbly stepped aside and let the Scripture captivate.

Okay, Lord. I told You I'm ready to learn. If that's what You're doing here, bring it on.

Almost immediately, he felt a prompt to speak. "I could hang around through next weekend and preach on Sunday, if you don't mind a roommate for a few more days." Noah stiffened, his eyes wide. Did he just say that? That he wanted to stay?

"Are you sure?" Dale's surprise seemed to match his own. "Of course, I'd be delighted to have you."

Am I sure? The man who'd been counting the days until he could escape felt his head bobbing up and down in the affirmative. "Absolutely."

Dale grinned. "Great. If I recall correctly, you have a sermon already prepared. The one you were going to deliver the weekend you arrived."

That seemed so long ago. "I do have a sermon. But if it's all right with you, I'd like to put it aside and pick up where you left off in Corinthians last week. You've got an incredible gift for opening Scripture and bringing the truths to life. One of the things I like best about your preaching is that you don't let your personality get in the way of the message."

"Thank you." He nodded modestly. "Your grandfather says you're an excellent speaker."

Noah shrugged. "Public speaking comes easily to me. But after listening to your sermons, I have the unpleasant conviction that my delivery overshadows the content."

"Style over substance?"

Noah grimaced with conviction. "Yeah. So, if you're willing, I want you to teach me." He paused, wondering whether to share his recent insight. If anyone understood, it would be Dale. "Full disclosure? I feel like God brought me here because He wants me to learn from you."

His host's easy smile and matter-of-fact nod said Noah's big discovery was not news to him. Had Dale and the Lord been talking about him behind his back?

"I know we don't have much time, but I'd like you to walk me through your whole sermon-writing process—from choosing the topic, to the final draft, to the delivery. After I give the sermon, I want you to critique me." He put down his fork to lean in, locking eyes with Dale. "I need you to be completely honest with me, to tell me what you'd do differently and why."

The older man sat in silence for a moment. Noah suspected he was praying over the request, as he knew Dale did with all his decisions. One more thing to emulate. At last, Dale nodded. "I'd be honored to teach you what I know."

Relief and a deep sense of assurance that he'd heard from God and responded in obedience flooded Noah. "Thank you."

"Lesson number one. I don't like to start with a topic, except on Mother's Day, Father's Day, Easter, and Christmas. Too easy to pick and choose scripture to support my viewpoint. Better to prayerfully select a book of the Bible and go through it verse by verse. That way you keep things in context and don't skip over the hard issues."

Conversation over dinner, which included two helpings of meat loaf for Noah, was lively. The discussion of sermon prep and biblical exposition carried them through the meal and cleanup, and on into the evening.

Hours later, Dale glanced at the clock, then stretched his arms over his head. "Good work, Noah, my boy." He pointed to his desk, where several commentaries and Bibles lay open. "I have truly enjoyed this, but it's getting late. I'd best call it a night and head off to bed if I'm going to be up at a reasonable hour in the morning."

Noah cocked a brow. "Hate to break it to you, but five thirty is not reasonable."

Dale laughed as he pushed to his feet. "It's an old habit."

Noah gathered his notes into a single pile and stood. "I'm not ready to turn in yet. If it's okay with you, I'll go over to the church and play the piano for a while."

"Good idea." His nod seemed a tad overenthusiastic. "You ought to call the doctor. You two could play a duet or something."

Noah sent him a side-eyed look, searching for evidence of overt matchmaking. Dale's expression remained disinterested.

Noah shook his head. "No, you said it yourself. It's late."

Dale made a scoffing sound. "For me, maybe. Not for a couple of thirty-year-olds."

"I don't know. We'll see." Though the idea of inviting her had already occurred to him, he kept the enthusiasm from his voice. No point in giving the old wannabe matchmaker ideas. "Good night, Dale."

As Noah headed to his room, he debated the wisdom of calling Emily and inviting her over. On the one hand, he missed her. He hadn't seen or spoken to her today. It would be wonderful to be together, to share a piano bench and a laugh. He wanted to hear about her day and talk to her about his.

On the other hand, experience told him that scratching an itch only made it itchier. Spending time with the doctor would create a desire to spend more time with her.

Not smart. Even with this latest extension, he'd leave town after his sermon on Sunday. The odds of seeing Emily once he was back in Houston were low.

A sudden pang caused him to rub a hand over his heart. All day, something had felt off. He missed seeing her face, hearing her voice. What would it be like when they were no longer together?

With so many available forms of communication, long-distance relationships were possible. But in his experience, the successful ones were based on an end date—a time when the couple would no longer be separated.

For the foreseeable future, she had a practice in Village Green, he had a ministry in Houston. There would be no end date for the doctor and him.

CHAPTER TEN

Emily drew her pajama-clad legs under her on the sofa as she pointed the remote at the TV screen and flipped through the channels, looking for something mindlessly enjoyable to occupy the hours before bed. Watching television was a relatively new indulgence. Previously, any free time had been devoted to study.

Even today, with exams and quizzes in her rearview mirror, she only turned it on as a last resort. She'd already cleaned the kitchen after dinner, reviewed her notes from today's patients, and read a couple articles in the latest medical journal.

The clock on the mantel said it was almost nine. She could go to bed, but experience told her she wouldn't fall asleep this early. She continued switching channels. She paused as a commercial with a mother and baby flitted across the screen, reminding her of Hallie's big news. How exciting to think her friend carried a precious new life.

Having come from a big family, Emily had always thought she'd have three or four children of her own one day. Boys, girls—it didn't matter. She just liked kids. It wasn't too late, she reasoned over the loud ticktock of her biological clock. The only real obstacle would be to find a husband.

Noah's face popped into her mind for the gazillionth time that day. She frowned. What was it about human nature that the one man most inaccessible to her would be the one she couldn't stop thinking about?

He wasn't her type. In a matter of days, he wouldn't be in her zip code.

No. Future. Here.

It didn't matter that she countered every thought of him with the cold reality he wasn't for her. He continued to dominate her thoughts.

The fact they'd spent a good part of yesterday together didn't help. In the morning they'd shared a pew and hymnal at church. And to her credit, though it was uphill work to focus on the sermon with Noah at her side, she felt she got a lot out of the message.

After the service, Dale and Noah invited her back to the parsonage for lunch. The two men had prepared lasagna and were eager for her to try it. If someone had told her Noah would be so proud, yet so unsure of his new cooking skills, that he'd hold his breath while waiting for her reaction to her first bite, she'd have laughed in their face. Such vulnerability would have been unheard of in the self-assured, sophisticated man she'd met weeks ago. Yet, that's exactly what happened. The look of pleasure and gratification on his face when she told him it was delicious was indelibly imprinted in her memory.

The threesome lingered long around the kitchen table, eating and laughing. She enjoyed watching the interaction between the two men. Such an unlikely combination, a simple old man and a worldly celebrity, yet the friendship between them was unmistakable.

After the dishes were cleaned and leftovers stowed away, they continued their conversation in Dale's cozy den. While Dale dozed, snoring softly on the recliner, she and Noah shared the sofa and whispered stories. She didn't leave until five o'clock.

Both men had urged her to remain, and though genuinely

tempted, the fear of overstaying her welcome propelled her out the door. Later, on her regular Sunday night call with her mom, she avoided mentioning Noah. Her mother had made her opinion of pursuing a man so far out of her league abundantly clear.

Yes. He was out of her league. In looks, experiences, everything. But he was so wonderfully normal and relatable in ways that superseded his too-good looks and celebrity status.

Her cell phone rang, and she dug it out from the cushions on the couch. Noah's name appeared on the screen, almost as though she'd summoned him with her thoughts.

"Hello?" Despite the surge in her blood pressure, she managed to answer in a cool, casual voice.

"Hey, Doc. I know it's late, but I wondered if you wanted to come over to the church and play piano."

"Yes." Nothing casual about the way she pounced on the invitation.

"Great. I'll pick you up in five minutes."

Five? Phone to her ear, she sprang up off the sofa and sprinted to her bedroom. "You don't have to do that. I can drive over."

He snorted derisively. "What kind of man lets a woman drive out to meet him at night?"

"A practical one." She pulled open a dresser drawer and pawed one-handed through the contents. "I don't mind driving. Really."

"Not happening. See you in a few."

After disconnecting the call, Emily scrambled out of her pajamas and into a clean white T-shirt and shorts. She slipped on a pair of flip-flops and ducked into the bathroom to get a peek at her reflection. *Hmm.* She eyed her freshly scrubbed face and nighttime braid with displeasure. Too bad she and Hallie hadn't had their Fort Worth excursion yet. She could do with a little polish right about now.

After locking up, she thundered down the metal stairs and stepped out through the exterior door opening into the parking lot. Joe had hung a light fixture above the exit that bathed the area in a large semicircle of warm, yellow light. Moths fluttered around it.

Seconds later, the headlights of Noah's Tesla appeared at the corner. He cruised over, stopping so the passenger door was directly in front of her.

"Hey." He flashed her a heart-stopping smile when she climbed into the car. "Glad you could make it."

"I'm glad you called." She pulled the seat belt across her lap and clicked it into place. "I had resorted to killing time in front of the television." *Anything to prevent me from daydreaming about you.*

"You should have called me." He steered the vehicle out of the parking lot onto the deserted street. "I'm always available to hang out with you."

Her heart soared with the knowledge. "I'll remember that." Of course, they didn't have much time left. And any time she spent with him only made it more difficult to put him out of her mind. "What have you been up to today?"

"Dale and I worked on the sermon I'm going to preach on Sunday—"

"That's nice," she responded automatically before his words could register." Once she realized what he'd said, she swiveled her face to his. "Wait! Did you just say you're preaching on Sunday?"

Eyes on the road, he nodded.

"Here?"

He glanced over, his wide grin illuminated by the dash lights. "Yeah."

"How in the world did he talk you into staying?"

"He didn't. I volunteered."

She scooted around in her seat, reached over, and pressed her palm to his forehead. "No fever."

He laughed as he pulled into the church parking lot. "I had the same reaction. I wanted to slap my hand over my mouth, but too late. I'd already committed."

Though he didn't look upset about another delay, she felt the need to offer comfort. "I'm sorry. Remind yourself it's just a couple more days." Tough to offer any genuine commiseration when the "Hallelujah Chorus" echoed through her brain.

He parked under one of the streetlamps, and they followed the sidewalk to the double front doors of the church. Noah slid the key into the lock and pushed open the right side of the door. He flipped on the lights in the sanctuary, and together they walked down the aisle and up onto the platform.

Emily paused before the altar with the simple wooden cross hanging on the wall behind it and sighed. "This is such a beautiful old church."

Noah continued on to the piano. After setting a hymnal on the music rack, he lifted his head, his gaze slowly sweeping the room. "It really is." He sounded surprised, as though he'd made a discovery. "I almost didn't notice."

She faced him with a laugh. "How could you miss it?"

He lifted his broad shoulders in a shrug. "I was blind, but now I see?"

They both laughed.

Noah pointed to the keyboard. "Do you want to play something solo, or should we try something together?"

No way she wanted to showcase her meager talent. "Since this was your idea, I think you should go first."

He pulled out the bench and sat. "Any requests?"

"Yes. Play something you love."

A smile stretched across his face, and he nodded. "Mozart, then." Leaning slightly forward, he lifted his hands to the keys and played.

She'd taken the chair Dale used to preach from and positioned it so she had an unobstructed view of Noah. With no written music to guide him, he performed the complicated piece from memory. He swayed as his long fingers moved effortlessly over the keys, coaxing the richest, full-bodied sounds from the baby grand. The music soared, swelling in her chest, in her spirit, and reverberating through the sanctuary.

The moment felt sacred, as though by his music Noah had ushered them into the very presence of the Almighty.

Emily was so caught up in the power and majesty that, as the last note faded, she whispered an amen.

Dropping his hands to his lap, he looked over at her and smiled. "It hits me the same way. Mozart wrote it as a secular piece, but it feels like high praise."

For a moment, she sat speechless. At last, she sighed. "Noah, you have such an incredible gift. I've never heard anything like it."

"Thank you. I had hoped to be a worship leader one day."

Had hoped. She heard disappointment, regret, even sorrow over unfulfilled dreams in his whisper. "I suppose, with your family legacy, you wouldn't have the opportunity to pursue a different path."

"No, it wasn't my family's decision. It was mine. I can't lead worship because I sing like a frog."

A giggle escaped before she remembered his refusal to sing at church. "Really? You're serious?"

He dipped his chin solemnly.

"I'm sorry you can't sing, but the fact is, you do lead worship."

He frowned. "How do you figure that?"

"Worship isn't just song. Jesus taught the importance of

worshipping in both spirit and in truth. I believe He was saying that worship takes place in the heart in response to knowledge. We praise and honor God because we know Him. By supplying people with knowledge of God through the truth of Scripture, you provide the crucial connection between the heart and mind. You are leading us in worship."

After a beat of thoughtful silence, a slow smile spread across his face. "Thank you."

"What for?"

He lifted his shoulders in a negligent shrug. "For being so wise. For hanging out with me tonight. For being you."

The warmth in his look brought heat to her cheeks. "You're welcome."

He shifted over on the bench and patted the newly vacated space. "Okay. It's your turn."

Noah watched the indecision move across her expressive face. His invitation rattled her, whether because she was uncomfortable about her talent or sharing a bench with him, he didn't know.

Calling her tonight had been a good move. Emily made everything better. Talking with her and getting her perspective made his world feel right. He was glad he'd invited her, even if it would make their inevitable separation more painful.

He patted the spot beside him again. "Come on, Doc. No welching. I played for you. Now you play something."

"It's not the same." She practically wrung her hands as she approached. "I feel silly performing for you when you're so much better than me."

"Not better. Different. You may play different types of pieces, but you perform with musicality and feeling."

She rolled her eyes. "Now I know you're just being nice." She lowered onto the bench and scooted to the very edge.

"Nope. I'm always honest with you." The revelation stopped him. As a man of God, he tried to be principled in all his dealings. But realistically, there were times when he fudged on the truth for the sake of expediency. Omitted information. Glossed over certain details.

He didn't want that with Emily. It mattered that everything between them be based in honesty.

"Thank you." She opened the hymnal. "What do you want me to play?"

He gave her the open invitation she'd given him. "Something you love."

Without hesitation, she set aside the hymnbook and raised her hands to the keys, playing a hauntingly familiar melody.

It took listening to several bars before he could place it. "Be Thou My Vision."

Smiling, she nodded as she finished the piece.

He shifted to face her. "You've been holding out on me, Doc. You played that from memory. I distinctly recall you saying you needed to read the music to play."

She ducked her head in an endearingly modest gesture. "Ordinarily I do. This piece is special. I play it whenever I need direction. The lyrics help center me." She shrugged. "I guess I've played it so much, I memorized it."

"I thought Dr. Cutler always knew where she was going."

She remembered telling him she'd known since childhood that she'd be a doctor one day. "I had the big picture, certainly, but I've had my share of angst in finding the details of my path."

One more thing they had in common. He nudged her. "Play something else."

"No more solos." Reaching across him, she pulled the discarded hymnal off the rack and opened it. "Let's find something we can do together."

They took turns picking songs. Since they shared the keyboard, Emily playing the treble clef while he took the bass, they sat hip to hip. He may have taken a bit more than his share of the bench. If she minded him crammed up against her, she didn't say so.

Personally, he thought it was great.

For one thing, she smelled wonderful. He didn't know when he'd come to prefer the light, fresh scent of soap over that of expensive perfume, but on the doctor it was perfect. And the soft warmth of her side pressed to his was both soothing and exciting.

"Did anyone ever tell you that you have beautiful hands?" *Oops.* Did he say that out loud?

She pulled them from the keys, burying them in her lap before giving him a frowning once-over. "For the second time tonight, I wonder if you are feverish."

He laughed. "And for the second time tonight, the words popped out of my mouth before I could stop them. I seem to have misplaced my filter. I'm sorry if I embarrassed you."

"Your delusions do not embarrass me." The fact she wouldn't look at him told a different story.

"Delusions?" He couldn't leave the challenge unmet, especially when her rejection of his compliment sounded sincere, as though she really didn't know how beautiful she was. "Give me your hand."

She tucked them between her thighs. "No."

He wiggled his fingers in invitation. "Come on, Doc. Give me your hand. I know you science types need proof. I'm going to give it to you."

She lifted her gaze, huffed out a long-suffering sigh, then reluctantly placed her palm against his.

He lifted it slightly, turning it from side to side in examination. "This hand is beautiful in both function and appearance." He adopted the lofty tone of a narrator on a wildlife documentary.

The corners of her mouth turned up in a look of patient amusement.

"I've witnessed these incredible appendages field a softball with impressive accuracy, tickle the ivories with true skill, and minister to the wounded with a light, compassionate touch."

"Thank you." She tried to pull her hand away.

He held firm. "I'm not finished. For all its strength and competence, this hand is surprisingly delicate." The description applied to all of Emily. She was amazingly tough, both mentally and physically, yet tenderhearted and spiritually sensitive. It rocked him to think how blessed and privileged he was to know her. His breath hitched and his chest tightened with emotion as he turned her hand and stroked a finger along the soft well of her palm. He looked into her blue eyes. "Infinitely precious."

Okay, now he was scaring himself. What was he getting worked up about? It was a hand, for heaven's sake. As a preacher, he'd shaken thousands of them over the course of his career, and, God willing, many thousands more to come in the years ahead.

Lighten up before she thinks you're nuts. He gave himself a mental shake.

"In conclusion, let me say your skin is as smooth as—well, I believe the phrase is as smooth as a baby's behind, but that never sounded much like a compliment to me."

"Enough." Laughing, she snatched her hand away. "Is it my turn to pick a hymn?"

The strange spell was broken, but Noah remained shaken.

What was going on? Never in his life had he become so emotional about a woman, much less a woman's hand. This was seriously scary stuff.

She leaned toward him, angling her face into his line of sight. "Noah?"

"What? Oh, yeah, sure." He smiled. "You choose."

Luckily, he could play accompaniment without focusing because his mind was anywhere but on the notes. As his fingers marched along with hers, his thoughts retraced earlier ground.

This evening, God had graciously shown him that his attitude stunk. Then, his study of Corinthians with Dale detailed exactly what a right attitude looked like. Love. Christ followers were to do everything in love.

By choosing to come to Village Green as an inconvenienced party, he'd acted in begrudging duty instead of love. A noisy gong. A clanging cymbal. A jerk. By the grace of God, he repented, received forgiveness, and moved on.

It appeared the lesson wasn't over.

Earlier tonight when Emily had pointed out the beauty of the sanctuary, he'd realized that by viewing everything through a lens of smug condescension, he'd almost missed the magnificence of the old structure. It wasn't the style he preferred, sleek and shiny with lots of glass and the newest technology, but there were beauty and holiness in the timeworn wood and stained glass.

Then there was his treatment of Emily. Within minutes of meeting, he'd dismissed her as beneath his consideration. How stupid could he be? He hated to think how close he'd come to missing her in his life.

For some reason, even in his contempt, she'd attracted him. Proximity and shared newcomer status played a role for sure, but there was more. Emily Cutler was bright, articulate, and fun. She made him think. She had his back. She got him. She was the most beautiful woman of his acquaintance, inside and out.

He stole a peek at her. With suddenly clear vision, the doctor looked like more than a friend. As the veil parted, he sensed he was looking at the woman of his dreams.

Wait! Whoa. He fumbled the notes. "Sorry." He glanced at the music, picking up where he'd stopped.

They'd known each other a whopping ten days. Sensible people didn't find the woman of their dreams in a matter of weeks. Especially when they weren't looking for love.

Love? Perspiration beaded his forehead as his panic escalated. Why was he even thinking about that kind of love? This wasn't the time or place for romantic entanglement. And this certainly wasn't how he planned it. She had commitments. He had commitments. She was staying. He was going.

"Wow, it's getting late."

Emily's gentle observation interrupted his spiraling thoughts. He shook his head to clear it. "Sorry, I lost track of time."

"Me too. But I'd better get home. Tomorrow starts early."

It couldn't be a good sign he didn't want to take her home or that he had an almost overpowering need to grab her hand and clasp it to his heart. He scrubbed his palms down his thighs instead. "I had fun tonight."

She gave him a shy smile. "Me too."

He continued to stare at her, making no attempt to stand. "We should do this again."

"I'd like that."

He didn't know how long they sat there, hip to hip, eye to eye, but he'd have been content to remain there forever.

Okay, lover boy. Take the poor woman home before you do or say something stupid. With a sigh, he pushed to his feet and stepped around the bench, waiting for her to precede him down the aisle.

He switched off the lights and locked up in careful silence. His mind was so full of crazy thoughts, he feared what would spill out if he opened his mouth.

They made the short trip back to Emily's apartment without speaking. Even silence with her was comfortable.

She pushed open her passenger door, then turned toward him before stepping out. "Is everything okay?"

"Yeah." His eyes were trained on the path of his headlights. "I've got a lot on my mind."

She lingered. "Can I help?"

"It's not a problem, exactly." Sighing deeply, he shifted to face her. "It's just that I . . . I really like you."

He heard her soft intake of breath. Even in the shadows of the car he could see her dark brows lift and her soft lips part in surprise.

He shook his head. "Sorry, that was—"

She reached out, placing a cool hand lightly on his forearm. "No, it's okay." She smiled. "I really like you too."

He felt a goofy grin settle over his face. *She really liked him.* He looked into her sea-blue eyes. "You're a very special person, Dr. Cutler."

Her smile stretched wider. "Thank you, Pastor Speers. I think you're very special too."

"We haven't known each other long—"

"—just a couple weeks."

"But I already feel deeply connected to you."

Eyes locked on his, she nodded in solemn understanding.

"I'm leaving in a few days."

Her smile dimmed as she nodded again.

"The ministry in Houston . . . I've been training for it all my life."

He saw her steel herself with a deep breath, infusing strength into her wobbly smile. "You'll be wonderful. I know God will use you mightily."

For once her knack for calm didn't make him feel any better. "Just as He will use you mightily in Village Green."

"I hope so."

"If I weren't leaving . . . "

She looked away.

He didn't need to go down that path. No point indulging in hopeless *what-ifs*. "Let me walk you to the door."

"It's not necessary."

But it was. Their time together slipped away like water through a sieve. He refused to waste a single drop they had left.

Side by side, they walked to the apartment entrance. A chorus of crickets and cicadas filled the silence while Emily keyed in a code and the lock clicked. He opened the metal door and stepped back for her to enter.

"I've got it from here." She pointed to the top of the stairs before smiling at him. "I'm glad you called. I had a really good time."

He caught her hand as she turned to go. She paused and looked up at him, a question on her face. He lifted her hand and pressed his lips to her knuckles. "I did too. Good night."

CHAPTER ELEVEN

Emily slid off her white coat and fitted it over the hanger. Two quick knocks sounded at the door, then Jodi poked her head into the office. "Oh, hey, Dr. Cutler. Are you leaving?"

Emily nodded. "I'm headed over to Estelle's. I'm meeting Pastor Speers and Dorcas Palmer for lunch."

Jodi scrunched up her face in a frown as she stepped into the room. "That's one weird combination. I mean, Pastor Speers I can see, but Dorcas Palmer?"

"Noah and Dorcas are big friends. I'm just tagging along."

"Which is also super strange. And kind of sweet. I know Dorcas and she's a real piece of work. Pastor Speers must be a very kind man to hang out with her."

"He is."

"Have fun."

"Thank you. I'll be back in time for my appointment at one fifteen."

"Okay, see you then."

Once her medical assistant had closed the door, Emily hurried to the mirror for a quick check before she headed out. Same boring ponytail, plain white blouse, and practical navy skirt. Smart, big-hearted Dr. Cutler.

She leaned in. Closer examination revealed a new light in her eyes, a fuller smile, a more confident tilt of her head—the earmarks of a woman who'd been singled out by the most wonderful man in the world.

Noah liked her. He really liked her.

Her pragmatic self recognized—even reluctantly accepted— that this was not the happily-ever-after, forever kind of bond. What she had with Noah was a crazy, inconvenient, inexplicable meeting of two hearts beating in harmony. A sweet interlude of kindred spirits soon to be separated by their divergent paths.

They didn't have a future. They had less than a week.

But Noah liked her. He *really* liked her. She bolstered her spirits with the thought every time reality tried to steal her joy. Next week, when he was gone, she'd grieve. Until then, she would wring every drop of pleasure from their fleeting time together.

She grabbed her bag from her desk drawer and exited the clinic through the employees-only door in the back. Though the temperature outside hovered in the high nineties, she chose to walk to Estelle's. They kept the clinic so frigid, it would take her the two-block stroll to thaw out before she stepped into the ice-cold air-conditioning in the restaurant. Besides, it was a great way to implement the advice she gave her patients to get some exercise and vitamin D.

Estelle greeted her at the cash register by the door. "Welcome, Dr. Cutler. Are you by yourself today?"

She shook her head. "I'm meeting Dorcas Palmer and Pastor Speers."

A bewildered expression, similar to the one she'd seen on her medical assistant minutes ago, crossed Estelle's face. "Dorcas hasn't stepped foot in here in years. It's nice of you to take an interest in her."

"It was Pastor Speers's idea."

The older woman's thin brows shot up. "Isn't that something? It's been my experience that folks as pretty and important as him don't usually have much to do with lesser folks. Of course, being a preacher and all, I expect he has to be nice to everyone."

Emily grinned. "I imagine it's strongly encouraged."

Estelle laughed. "Go ahead and find a table you like, and I'll bring your drink. Tea or Dr Pepper today?"

Emily usually limited herself to a soda in the afternoon, but today she felt like splurging. "Dr Pepper, please." Spotting a centrally located, open table, she moved in that direction.

"Hey, Dr. Cutler." The Ryders, an older couple from church, waved her over.

She stopped at their table. "Hi."

"Are you all alone? We'd love for you to join us." Mrs. Ryder pointed to an extra chair beside her as she issued the invitation.

"Thank you." Emily glanced over her shoulder toward the entrance. "Actually, I'm meeting Pastor Speers and Dorcas Palmer."

"Pastor Speers?" Mrs. Ryder's voice rose with curiosity while her eyes lit with an unholy light. She gave Emily a searching look. "I was just telling Mr. Ryder that I'd never seen such a handsome preacher." Another look.

Pretty clear where the older woman was headed with this, but Emily wouldn't turn down any opportunity to talk about her favorite subject. "He's very handsome."

Mrs. Ryder cocked her head. "And single, I believe."

"Yes, ma'am. He is."

"How convenient. I mean him being single and you being single."

Mr. Ryder huffed out a breath as he threw his hands in the air. "Oh no, here she goes." He glared at his wife. "Simmer down, Jane. As I recall, Dale told us the young fella is just here for a brief visit."

She sniffed her displeasure at his interference. "Maybe he's changed his mind."

Mr. Ryder shook his head. "The doc here isn't interested in you setting her up with someone who lives in Houston." To Emily he added, "Jane fancies herself a matchmaker. Of course, there's another word for it. Busybody."

Emily stifled a laugh. "Matchmaking is an old and honorable profession."

"Mercy, Doc. Don't encourage her."

This time she did laugh. "I won't." She sent Mrs. Ryder a conciliatory smile. "But if I'm ever looking for Cupid's help, I'll know who to come to."

On her short trek to the table, she stopped three more times to speak with patients or people from church. Everyone in Village Green had made her feel so welcome. If Noah wouldn't be miles away, the little town would be absolutely perfect.

Even as she thought of him, he appeared in the entrance, tiny Dorcas at his side. He looked so handsome, if a bit overdressed for the blue-jeans crowd, in his crisply pressed shirt and slacks. He spotted Emily before she could signal to him.

Their progress across the room was as slow as hers had been.

"I feel like a celebrity." Dorcas's cloudy blue eyes glowed with pleasure when she and Noah finally arrived at the table. "I don't know why movie stars are always complaining. It's grand to have people make a fuss over you."

Noah winked at Emily as he pulled out the chair across from her for Dorcas and seated her. He settled into the place between them. "Hi, Doc. Been waiting long?"

"No, I just got here." She forced her eyes from his smile to include Dorcas in the conversation. "Did you two have a nice trip into town?"

Dorcas beamed. "We did indeed. The preacher here came to get me in his fancy car." She darted a look to her left and right, then lowered her voice. "I wouldn't tell anyone else, but he speeds."

Emily received the information with a solemn nod. "He's fortunate to have you to protect his reputation."

"We're friends," Dorcas confided as she waved a gnarled hand between her and Noah. "We like to get together for lunch. When he asked me out, I didn't realize you'd be joining us." Her expression turned sly. "He hadn't mentioned he had a sweetheart."

Emily felt her face heat. "Oh, no, we're not sweethearts."

Dorcas placed her hands on the table and leaned in to give her a hard stare. "My eyesight isn't what it used to be, missy, but it's as clear as the nose on your face that you two have what is known as a *thing*."

For a small person, the older woman's voice carried. And the way she said "thing" implied something unsavory. Emily's cheeks flamed hotter. "What? Oh, no, ma'am. No thing. Just friends."

"Very *good* friends," Noah supplied with a chuckle, clearly enjoying Emily's discomfort.

Dorcas shrugged her narrow shoulders. "Whatever you say. Just remember"—she pointed a finger at Emily, then Noah—"no sex before marriage."

Heads popped up all over the restaurant. No one could have missed her trumpeted declaration. Emily jerked the menus from behind the napkin dispenser and practically tossed them at Noah and Dorcas. For the sake of everyone who now watched their little party, she planted a smile on her face. "What does everyone want for lunch?"

"The special looks good." The self-conscious look on Noah's face said he was no longer amused.

"There's no cause to be embarrassed." Dorcas laid down her

menu, refusing to be distracted from her topic. "I remember being young and having my head full of sex. I'm sure it's all the hormones. No sin in having hormones, is there, Pastor?"

He cleared his throat. "Nope. None at all."

"But having sex outside of marriage, now that's a sin. The Bible calls it forn-i-cation," she added helpfully, at the top of her lungs. "Ain't that right, Preacher Man?"

He slunk down in his chair as he glanced around the suddenly quiet room. "Yes."

Emily cleared her throat and leaned in to prevent her words from broadcasting. "I wonder, Dorcas, would it be okay with you if we change the subject?"

"Sure, if it makes you uncomfortable." The old woman turned to Noah. "Seems odd for a doctor to be squeamish about sex. It's natural, you know."

"That's true, it is natural," Noah answered, "but I have to agree with Emily. It doesn't seem like the best topic for lunch conversation."

Mercifully, Dorcas silenced.

As the three of them studied their menus, Emily risked a peek at Noah. She caught his eye and he grinned, lifting his brows in acknowledgment of the awkwardness.

"I think I'll have the fried chicken." Dorcas placed her menu on the table. "Nobody makes it better than Estelle."

Noah nodded. "Me too."

"Fried chicken sounds good to me." Emily collected the menus and tucked them behind the napkin dispenser.

Estelle arrived to take their order. "Just so you know, your lunches are on the house."

Noah shook his head. "Oh, no. We don't want you to do that."

"Absolutely." She smiled at Dorcas over the top of her half

glasses. "It's been a long while since Dorcas has been in the restaurant. Seeing an old friend is cause for celebration."

Dorcas flushed with pleasure. "Thank you. That's mighty kind."

"Yes, thank you." Noah spread his arms to encompass the table. "We've all settled on the fried chicken, mashed potatoes, and green beans."

Nodding, Estelle tucked the notepad in her apron. "Got it. I'll have it out for you in no time."

Dorcas waited until the owner was on the other side of the restaurant before clapping with childlike delight. "Free lunch. *Whooee.* I bet even movie stars don't get free lunch. I think we should order dessert, too, since it won't cost us nothing."

The three of them chatted while they waited for their meals. Emily steered the conversation to neutral topics—the endless Texas heat, the Rangers' chances for making the playoffs, the deplorable state of the roads. Noah helped ensure the talk flowed in acceptable G-rated channels.

Emily loved to watch him. The play of emotions across his beautiful face fascinated her. A slight furrowing of his brow when he listened, the way he compressed his lips as he considered his reply, the way he threw his head back and laughed at something silly Dorcas had said. She could watch him for hours.

Today she paid extra close attention, storing away each precious detail. Honestly, what she really wanted was to pull out her phone and record him so she could replay it over and over after he was gone.

"Three fried chicken lunches." Estelle returned to deliver their plates and refill their drinks. "I'll check back in a while."

"Let me ask a quick blessing, and we'll eat."

They joined hands. While Noah prayed over their meal, Emily

added a silent request that she be able to remember exactly how it felt to have her palm cradled in his.

"Amen." With a discreet squeeze, he released her. "So, Doc, how's business today?"

"The clinic's been busy. Every week I see an increase in patients."

Dorcas picked up a drumstick and took a big bite. "We're all so glad to have a doctor in town again." She spoke and chewed simultaneously. "It's been tough, especially for us old folks, to drive into Corsicana for every ache and pain. Back in the day, we had a doctor and a dentist."

When she stopped talking to swallow, Noah turned to Emily. "Dorcas is a lifelong resident of Village Green. She claims it was quite a bustling metropolis back in the day."

Emily nodded. "I can believe that. It's a lovely town."

"A few years ago, I would have said we were through." Dorcas took another big bite of chicken. More noisy chewing. "Businesses were closing, old people dying, and young folks leaving to find work. Village Green got to looking like a ghost town. Then, about a year or so ago, the mayor and chamber of commerce got busy coming up with activities and events to draw in the tourists and turn things around. The way I hear it, that's how we got the bakery next door, and the new first-grade teacher at the elementary school. Now, with the doctor here, that makes three young people moving into the area."

Emily thought of her friend. "I believe Hallie Gunther moved back within the last year or two."

"You're exactly right." Dorcas sent Noah a side-eyed glance and sly grin. "Who knows who'll be next."

He shook his head. "Not me." He gave Emily a warm smile. "Though while I admit Village Green has grown on me, my job is waiting for me back in Houston."

Dorcas bobbed her head. "I remember. You're the pastor who doesn't visit his church members."

His sigh told Emily this wasn't the first time they'd had this conversation. "In a very large church, we delegate responsibility. Everyone does what they're best at."

"So you keep saying." She wagged the now-clean drumstick at him. "Fact is, you do a fine job at visitation."

He dipped his chin humbly. "Thank you."

Dorcas dropped the bone on her plate and stuck her finger in her mouth. "The doc and I are going to miss you when you're gone."

Noah smiled across the table at the diminutive woman who was so short, she was only visible from the neck up. Unfortunately, that was enough that he couldn't unsee the finger she had stuffed in her mouth, working busily to dislodge something from her back teeth. "I'll miss you too."

He uttered the expected little white lie with convincing pastoral sincerity before realizing it was true. For some reason known only to God, he'd developed a genuine affection for this atrocious, potty-mouthed old woman who picked her teeth in public and spoke her mind at a half shout. He'd worry about her when he was gone.

As he'd pulled up in front of her house this morning, he'd wondered who would take her out after he left. Dale visited her regularly, but he wasn't a young man. One day, in the not-too-distant future, he'd need someone to visit him. Emily would check on Dorcas if he asked her to, but she was busy building her practice.

While climbing the rickety stairs, he worried about her death-trap front porch. How long before she or some hapless visitor fell through one of the rotting boards?

"Did Pastor Speers mention he's preaching on Sunday?" Emily asked Dorcas.

Dorcas pulled her spitty finger from her mouth and swiveled her head toward him. "Is that right? Well, I hope these da—, er darn knees won't act up so I can get myself to church and hear what a big-city preacher sounds like." She frowned. "I hope my car will start. It's been a while since I had it out."

"You drive?" His voice ended with a squeak. *Oh, great.* Something else to worry about.

Emily shook her head. "If you need a ride, I'd be happy to pick you up."

His gaze drifted, settled on the doctor's face as she listened to Dorcas's prattle. Her blue eyes were trained on the older woman, her pretty lips turned up in a smile over something Dorcas said.

Emily was as strong and competent as any woman he knew, yet sweetly humble. She was crazy smart but never needed to push her considerable knowledge forward. She was perfect.

Last night, it had struck him how very much he would miss her.

As he lay in bed awaiting sleep, he'd had a heart-to-heart with the Lord. In his years as a believer, Noah had come to realize God didn't do anything without a purpose.

So where did this perfect woman fit into his life?

Was she there, at this critical juncture, to help him see himself more clearly? He'd teased her about being a conduit for self-intro-spection. Something about the clear-eyed gaze she leveled on him made him want to see what she was seeing. To get a true picture of who he was so he could enact the changes necessary to transform him into the man God called him to be.

Emily was the first woman he could envision spending his life with. But she was contractually obligated and wholeheartedly com-mitted to serving here for the next four years. If he wanted to be with her, he'd have to relocate to Village Green. Which meant turning his back on his birthright, his family, and everything he'd worked for.

Maybe she was some sort of test, a lovely distraction used by God to measure his dedication to his calling, his devotion to the Lord's service.

He was probably reading too much into it. Maybe she was just a like-minded companion God had graciously provided to walk alongside him in a lonely stretch of life. In which case, the Almighty had gone over and above with his selection of Emily. He'd sent a woman so perfect that Noah didn't want her companionship for a few weeks. He wanted to walk with her for a lifetime.

He fell asleep without receiving an answer to his questions.

Or maybe he had. No matter the reason she figured so prominently in his present, there was no place for her in his future.

Emily's landlords, Joe and Eden, and their son Jake stopped by the table as everyone was finishing up. "Hey, y'all." Eden smiled. "We saw you come in and thought we'd say hello."

"I'm glad you did." Emily nodded toward Dorcas. "Do you know Dorcas Palmer?"

"We do." Joe nodded, sending the old woman a smile. "It's great to see you out and about, Ms. Palmer."

Dorcas lowered her snow-white head in a regal nod. "Thank you. I'm having a fine time. Estelle gave us our lunch for free."

"That's cool." Joe looked to Noah. "How's your arm? All healed up from the game?"

"Good as new." A thought sprang to mind, and in what was rapidly becoming a habit, he spoke before he considered it long enough to talk himself out of it. "Do I remember you saying you do construction?"

Joe shrugged. "Yeah."

Noah hitched a thumb toward Dorcas. "I noticed my friend has some bad boards on her front porch. What would it take for me to repair them?"

Joe cocked a brow, his expression frankly skeptical. "You know anything about working with wood, Preacher?"

Noah hunched his shoulders. "I took out a splinter once."

Joe laughed. "Tell you what. I've got some free time on Friday. Why don't you and I run out to Ms. Palmer's place and take a look at what needs doing."

Whew. While he hadn't been fishing for an offer of help, he certainly welcomed it. "I'd appreciate it."

Joe gave him a quick once-over, then frowned. "I'll bring you something to wear to work in. Eden would have a fit if I let you mess up your nice clothes."

Noah fought the urge to roll his eyes. Why was everyone so worried about his wardrobe? "Sure, man. Thanks."

Joe wrapped his arm behind his wife and son. "We need to get going. Time for Jake's nap. Great to see you all."

Emily waited until they were out of earshot before leaning toward Noah, her hand pressing lightly on his forearm. *"You're* going to fix Dorcas's porch?"

Because it was a legitimate question, he couldn't be insulted by the incredulity in her eyes or the concern in her voice. She probably worried she needed to be on standby at the clinic in case he injured himself, which, honestly, was not outside the realm of possibility. Since he didn't have the first idea about carpentry, he wasn't sure why he'd volunteered for the job.

Blame it on Corinthians. The text for Sunday's sermon continued to play through his mind. Funny thing about Scripture—any time spent in the Word to prepare a message for others invariably ended up impacting him. The passage from Corinthians hit him squarely between the eyes. To walk in biblical love meant action.

Instead of shaking his head over the rotten boards, or worrying about Dorcas falling through the porch, he needed to do something about it.

When love saw a need, love acted.

God bless Joe for volunteering to help. While Noah knew nothing about woodworking, Joe did. Between them they could make the necessary repairs and keep Noah's new old friend safe.

Emily sent him a look of such unadulterated admiration, it warmed him to his toes. "You're a good man, Noah Speers."

He wanted to be the person she saw when she looked at him, to be the man worthy of the esteem she bestowed on him, but since owning up to his tendency toward selfishness, he was now wholly aware that any good thing in him was a direct gift of grace.

"Yes, he is." Dorcas pulled her finger from her mouth to point the moist appendage at him. "And you'd make a fine replacement for Dale when he retires."

Emily straightened in surprise. "Is Dale retiring?" She directed the question to Noah.

This was news to him. "Not that I've heard."

Dorcas nodded confidently. "He's mentioned it several times to me. The poor man is eighty. He's earned the right to retire."

"Of course, he has." The doctor spoke with sympathetic compassion. "So why doesn't he?"

Dorcas shrugged. "Nobody to take his place. He loves the old church and would hate to see it shut down, so he stays."

Emily's distressed expression mirrored his feelings. "That's terrible."

"A da—er, durn shame. Especially when we have the perfect replacement for him right here." She turned, batting her rheumy eyes at Noah and giving him a crooked smile.

Him? Stuck in Village Green? No way. "Ha ha. Nope. If you will recall, I have a job waiting for me back in Houston."

"Yes, but they don't need you like we do." The old woman looked to Emily for confirmation.

"My family might disagree."

Dorcas eyed him expectantly, as though waiting for him to supply a solution.

He cleared his throat. "But I can certainly help. My father and grandfather know everybody. With their connections, I'm sure we can find a replacement. I'll talk to Dale about it, and if he's interested, I'll speak to my dad."

Noah broached the topic over dinner.

Dale put down his fork and sighed. "It's true. I've given retirement some thought. I've even had a committee look into finding a replacement for me."

Putting it to committee sounded like *serious* thought. "And?"

The older man gave him a shadowed smile. "You of all people won't be surprised to hear we haven't been able to attract any viable candidates." His weary sigh made him sound every bit of his eighty years. "It's a small congregation, so we can't afford to pay much salary, and the town's predominantly older population doesn't show much potential for growth. The chamber of commerce has been working to attract young people, but it's tough going. Folks need jobs and something to do. Not much of either in Village Green. It'll take a miracle."

Amen. Beyond low pay and an elderly population, there was the town itself. Who in their right mind would volunteer to bury themselves in this tired old relic of a town? Emily's face popped into Noah's mind.

"In the meantime, I'm good." Dale picked up his fork and speared a bite of casserole. "I think of Paul and remember I can do all things through Christ who strengthens me."

Noah watched the older man eat, his own appetite gone. He hated to think of his mentor and friend struggling beneath the load he carried. "Do you mind if I talk with my father and grandfather about it? They have connections everywhere. Maybe they could send a replacement your way?"

Dale smiled. "I don't mind at all. I know the committee would be grateful for some leads. But I don't want you to worry. I have absolute faith when the timing is right, God will provide."

CHAPTER TWELVE

Noah got up with the sun. Nerves about his sermon and mixed feelings about leaving town, specifically Emily, propelled him from the cozy double bed at first light.

After a prayer asking God to speak to him through His Word, he picked up his Bible from the nightstand and, sitting on the edge of the mattress, began to read in Psalms. "Delight yourself in the Lord and he will give you the desires of your heart."

The familiar passage took on new meaning this morning. In the past, he'd understood it to mean that, as a reward for abiding in God, God would give him what he wanted.

Today it seemed to say that as he focused on loving and serving God, He would in turn mold Noah's desires to line up with what God wanted for him.

Noah's thinking underwent a subtle yet important shift. In that moment, he went from desiring to please himself to wholeheartedly surrendering to what God wanted for his life.

The Bible was replete with assurances that his heavenly Father wanted and worked for good in the lives of His children. Noah's years of experience walking with Him confirmed it. God was good, therefore Noah could trust Him with his life. Even the painful stuff.

With the clarity of hindsight, he now knew this "detour" he'd made to Village Green to help out his grandfather's old friend wasn't an unscheduled bump in the road, but rather a deliberate move scripted by the Almighty to instruct and refine him.

Though he didn't yet see the reason for the introduction of Emily into his life when they were moving in opposite directions, he trusted that in time he would understand. And that through it all, God would direct Noah's desires to match His own.

Thirty minutes later, showered and dressed, Noah walked into the kitchen. "Good morning." He sniffed deeply. "Smells good in here. I thought we agreed you wouldn't cook this morning."

Dale sat at the table, a cup of coffee in his hand. He sent Noah a sheepish smile. "I know, but I wanted you to have a substantial breakfast, since you were preaching." He glanced at the clock on the wall. "You're up early. Some of my bad habits must have worn off on you."

"I sincerely hope so." Noah grabbed a cup from the cabinet and filled it from the pot on the coffee maker before taking a seat across from the older man. "I can't think of a better man to emulate."

Dale met his eyes over the rim of his cup. "Thank you."

"I mean it. I've learned more from you in two weeks than I've learned throughout college and divinity school." He lifted his coffee in a toast. "To a brief but profitable mentorship. I'm truly grateful."

"I've benefited as well. I've enjoyed having someone to cook with. And our discussions of Scripture have given me new insight. I'll miss you." Dale paused. "As will the doctor."

"I'm telling myself that once I'm gone, and she and I return to our normal routines, this . . ."—he groped for the right word—". . . *thing* will fade like a summer-camp romance. Some nice memories. That's all."

The older man didn't look any more convinced than Noah felt. "I suppose it's possible."

Noah blew out a breath. "Here's the deal. There's no future for

Emily and me. None. We'll be three hours apart, which isn't so bad, but my busiest days are the ones she's off work and vice versa." He picked up the serving spoon and scooped a mound of the sausage egg casserole onto his plate. "She could come to Houston for the weekends, my parents would love to have her, but I wouldn't be able to spend much time with her. I could drive to Village Green in the middle of the week, but she'd be tied up at the clinic."

Dale nodded.

"I've done the math. An hour or two a week doesn't sound like the foundation of a lasting relationship. And relying on phone calls for the next four years doesn't sound promising, either."

"It appears you've given it a great deal of thought."

Noah scrubbed his hands over his face. "You have no idea. Emily is an incredible woman. I've never met anyone like her. She's smart, she's beautiful, she's . . ." He sighed. "It's obvious she's not for me. The timing, the circumstances, everything makes a relationship between us impossible."

"Have you talked to Emily about it? About how you feel?"

Noah shook his head. "Not really. What would I say? 'Emily, I've fallen in love with you after knowing you two whole weeks'?"

Dale chuckled. "Crazier things have happened."

"Not to me. She'd think I'm nuts. Honestly, I think I'm nuts. And even if what I feel for her is love and not just profound gratitude for her friendship at a critical time, what can I do about it? I can't give up my job, and she can't give up hers."

"It's certainly a quandary." Dale's gentle smile shone with hope. "But I'm reminded of the scripture that nothing is impossible with God."

"You're right. And I've got to believe that somewhere down the line, He'll show us what it was He wanted us to learn through our time together."

*   *   *

While Dale put the finishing touches on the roast cooking in the Crock-Pot for lunch, Noah walked over to the church. Bible in hand, suit jacket carefully folded and draped over his shoulder, he made his way along the concrete path bisecting the field between the parsonage and the church. The only sounds this time of day were the wind rustling the leaves in the trees and the gentle buzz of insects in the grass.

When he'd first arrived in town, the near total silence oppressed him. To a city boy, all the wide-open spaces and blanketing quiet gave him a serious case of the creeps. He needed the noise of traffic and people to feel alive.

This morning, the quiet sheltered and soothed. He appreciated the opportunity to be alone with his thoughts.

He followed the sidewalk around the side of the wooden building up to the double front doors of the church. He unlocked them and let himself in, switching on the lights as he went.

Sunlight filtered through the old stained glass windows in the sanctuary, gilding the room with an otherworldly light. So strong was the presence of God, Noah stopped halfway down the aisle, slipped into a pew, and bowed his head in reverence.

Heart filled with awe and gratitude, he thanked God for the privilege of being called His child, and the commission to teach others His truth. There on the old wooden pew, smoothed to a glossy sheen from decades of use, Noah rededicated himself to the Lord's service. He asked that God's desires would be his own, and for the strength to see it through, whatever the cost.

The door in the front of the sanctuary, behind the altar, opened with a creak and Trey Gunther peeked his head in. "Oh, hey, Noah. Sorry to bother you. I didn't know anyone was in here. I just finished making the coffee and I thought I'd check to be sure everything is open before I head home."

Noah lifted a hand in a friendly wave. "No problem."

Trey backed out. "I'll leave you and the Lord to your conversation."

Noah stood and moved down the carpeted aisle toward him. "No need. I think He and I are all caught up."

Trey met him halfway and shook his hand. "I've always thought this is a great place to connect with God. I know He's everywhere, but for some reason it's easier to hear Him in here."

Noah glanced around the room. "I agree."

Trey gave him a broad smile. "Hey, thanks for taking care of Dorcas's porch. That was really nice of you. I talked to Joe yesterday and he said the two of you were over there tearing out rotten boards and replacing them."

Noah grinned. "Did he also tell you I was less help than a two-year-old? That I know absolutely nothing about carpentry?"

Trey laughed. "Actually, no. He was impressed you were willing to tackle the job. And embarrassed that it took an out-of-towner to notice the need and get it done." He frowned. "Folks in Village Green pride ourselves on looking out for our own."

Noah lifted his shoulders in dismissal. "Everybody is busy. It happens."

Trey's smile returned. "I wish I'd known y'all were doing it. I just sat around all day since the girls went shopping."

"The doc mentioned she and Hallie were going to hit the town." Noah chose not to add that he hadn't been too pleased when Emily told him her plans, that he'd had to fight resentment over Hallie taking some of his precious time with the doctor.

Trey grinned. "Hallie was thrilled to find a pal to shop with.

There's never been a store my wife didn't like. Have you seen Emily since they've been back?"

"No. I was working on my sermon."

"You're going to be impressed." Trey's cell phone chimed. He pulled it from his pocket, checked the screen. "Hallie's texting she's ready for me to come get her." He typed in something, then slid the phone back in his pocket. "We'll be back in a bit. Looking forward to hearing you preach."

"Thanks. See you later." After waving Trey off, Noah retrieved his coat from the pew and walked to the simple oak pulpit he'd use when he delivered his sermon. As he laid his notes on the polished surface, he thought of all who'd gone before him, those who'd stood in the very same spot to share God's unchanging Word. What an incredible and humbling privilege to be part of the history.

His thoughts turned to Dale, who'd shepherded the congregation so faithfully his whole life. *"Lord, help me find him a replacement. Someone who will love these people as he has. Someone who loves Your Word and can teach it to others."* Noah paused before adding the most difficult part of the request. *"Send someone who can love this backwater town. It's a tall order, I know, but as Dale reminded me earlier, nothing is impossible with You."*

A glance at his watch said the first arrivals for Sunday school weren't due for another half hour. He had some time to play the piano and get his head and heart ready to deliver the message.

Like a kid at Christmas, Emily had been up with the sun on Sunday morning so she could play with all her new stuff. First stop after climbing out of bed was the bathroom mirror. Excitement about her makeover had made it hard to fall asleep last night. Would the changes appear as wonderful this morning?

She flipped on the light. Yes! She turned her head from side to side, reveling in hair that now hit several inches past her shoulder rather than past her waist. The straight cut wasn't fancy, but without the weight of the additional inches, it looked healthier and fuller. She watched her reflection as she swished it again. Dare she say *classy*?

Hands on the edge of the sink, she leaned in to examine her brows. By now, the redness had disappeared, leaving thick yet polished arches. Natural, but better. Who knew eyebrows made such a difference?

After she'd showered and dried her hair—amazing how quickly it dried—she headed to her closet to select one of her new dresses to wear to church. She and Hallie had found three that fit the agreed-upon criteria—simple, comfortable, and polished. Because the rest of her wardrobe was predominantly navy and white, Hallie suggested they add color.

The three dresses hung side by side: one fuchsia, one red, and one sapphire blue. Though all were similar in style—knee length with short sleeves—it didn't take her long to select the perfect one for church.

She slid the blue dress over her head and smoothed it over her hips. Both Hallie and the saleswoman raved about how the sheath fit like it was tailor-made for her, and how perfectly it matched the color of her eyes.

On more than one occasion, Noah had mentioned how striking her blue eyes were. On this, their last day together, she wanted to make sure he remembered her and her blue eyes.

Their last day together.

Tears welled. Good thing she'd vetoed mascara. She wanted to be memorable, but not for having ugly black streaks running down her cheeks.

She'd known this day was coming. From the beginning, she'd tried to keep him at arm's length, to protect her heart. She'd kept her expectations low, frequently reminding herself he was a gift from God with an expiration date. She was staying, he was going.

Obviously, she'd failed. But really, how did anyone protect themselves from a man like Noah? He was so funny, kind, wonderful—so Noah—how could she help falling for him?

Now, he was leaving. And she'd promised herself she would not make a scene, no matter how badly she wanted to. She would act with dignity. She would not sob uncontrollably or throw herself at his feet. She would not hide his keys, disable his car, or try in any way to prevent him from leaving.

She would not make him swear to call.

Instead, she would thank him for his friendship and wish him Godspeed. And after she waved him off with a serene smile on her face, she would return to her apartment and cry her eyes out.

Noah sat at the baby grand and, after shifting to settle in on the wooden bench, began to play. Chopin today. It didn't feel quite right without Emily at his side. Every night this week, with the exception of yesterday, when he was putting the final touches on his sermon and she was hanging out with Hallie, they'd shared the bench and music and the details of their lives. Sometimes they talked and laughed over the hymns, while other times they let the lyrics and notes do the talking.

At all times, he'd been hyperaware of his companion. The sound of her laughter, the scent of her hair, the warmth of her side pressed to his—all were indelibly imprinted in his memory. A question replayed through his mind. Would those impressions be enough to sustain him in the coming days?

The music segued into a minor key, taking his mood along with it. Emily had become so important to his happiness, so essential to his well-being. What would he do without her?

"I thought I'd find you here."

"Emily?" He pulled his hands from the keys, turning sharply in the direction of her voice.

She moved into his line of sight and, smiling, lowered onto the bench beside him. "No, don't stop. Finish the piece. It's lovely."

He took a moment to study her. His mouth went dry. "Speaking of lovely. Wow."

What had she done to herself? He couldn't put a finger on any specific changes—she looked like his Emily—only better. "You look amazing."

He dragged his eyes from her and resumed playing, but only because she asked, and at a galloping tempo that would have made the composer's head spin.

After the last chord, he swiveled to face her and gave a low whistle. "Did I mention that you look incredible? I mean it, Doc. You look . . ." Words failed him. "Wow."

Obviously embarrassed by his effusive praise, she lowered her eyes, her long lashes fanning across the pretty pink blush staining her cheeks. "Thank you. Hallie and I went into Fort Worth do some shopping, and while we were there, we made a stop at her salon." She reached up, touching the side of her head. "I got my hair cut."

"I see that." He allowed himself the luxury of a leisurely perusal. Her long, practical braid had been replaced with a slick fall of gleaming silk. He lifted a strand, rubbing it between his fingers. "It looks beautiful."

"And they fixed my eyebrows."

He frowned, having long since decided her strong brows were perfect. "I didn't know they were broken." Further inspection revealed the cosmetician managed to tame the thick, dark arches without destroying any of their natural beauty.

"And they had a makeup artist . . ."

He lifted a hand in protest. "Hold on, now. You don't need makeup."

Emily's face fell. "Does that mean you don't like my lipstick?"

"Like it?" He made a quick study of her mouth. Like it? He loved it. Suddenly all he could think about was how nice it would be to lean over and kiss those glossy pink lips. He resolutely turned his gaze to the stained glass panels behind her. "Very nice."

"You don't sound impressed."

He glanced over to see her lower lip protruding in a tempting pout. "Believe me. If I were any more impressed, we wouldn't be talking." He cleared his throat. "I thought you were picking up Dorcas this morning."

"I am. I stopped by the parsonage on my way to her house, to wish you luck. Dale told me you were here."

He placed a hand over hers resting in her lap. "I'm really glad you came."

Her beautiful blue eyes scanned his face. "Nervous about your sermon?"

"No." *Sad because I'll be leaving you.* "Just thinking about all the fun we've had."

Her hair swept forward over her shoulders as she nodded. "I can honestly say I haven't played the piano or laughed so much in my entire life."

"And I've never spent as much time soul-searching as I have

since meeting you." His gaze locked with hers. "You've been good for me."

She lowered her eyes, her glossy pink smile strained. "That sounds like a goodbye."

"No." He forced up the corners of his mouth while injecting optimism into his tone. "No way. We'll talk . . ."

"Sure." She bobbed her head. "That's what cell phones are for." Once again, their gazes held. "Right?"

Their half-hearted laughter faded into silence.

"I guess I'd better be going," Emily said. "Dorcas will wonder what's keeping me."

Noah stood when she did and moved around the bench. "Dale wanted me to ask you to come for lunch if you don't have other plans."

Her only plans were to spend every last minute with him, even if it meant inviting herself over. Thankfully, his offer saved her from the embarrassment. "Sounds great. I'll take Dorcas home after church and meet you at the parsonage."

"Perfect." Instead of meeting her eyes, he seemed to be staring at her lips again. "See you then."

Dorcas waited for her on the porch. She gave a cheery wave when Emily pulled up to the house and climbed out of the car. "Come up here and see what your Preacher Man has done."

Her Preacher Man. If only.

Dorcas extended her bony arms, proudly showing off her new porch and stairs. "See how sturdy they are?" She tapped her beige crepe-soled shoe on the new boards. "Noah and Joe worked the whole day. I tried to feed them, but they didn't want me to fuss."

More likely, Noah had warned Joe about the tuna.

"They picked up lunch at Estelle's and we had a nice picnic. They were still working at suppertime but wouldn't hear of me cooking. Said they didn't want to trouble me." Dorcas placed a gnarled hand over her heart. "Doesn't that beat all?"

"It's very sweet."

Dorcas heaved a sigh. "I'm gonna miss that preacher."

Emily's tears were back, hovering behind her eyelids. "Me too."

Dorcas turned a sympathetic gaze to her. "Did you ask him to stay? I bet he would if you asked."

Emily paused a moment, tilting her eyes skyward to regain her composure before shaking her head. "No, he has a job waiting for him in Houston."

The older woman *tsk*ed. "They don't need him as much as we do."

Truer words had never been spoken.

They arrived back at the church before Sunday school let out, giving them their choice of seats in the empty sanctuary. Emily tried to direct them to an inconspicuous spot, somewhere in the middle of the room.

"No. Let's sit up here so he can see us." Dorcas continued down the aisle to the very first pew and scooted along until she was directly in front of the pulpit. She patted the seat beside her in invitation. "This is the perfect spot."

Emily gulped. If by *perfect* Dorcas meant Noah couldn't miss them, she was correct. They were so close, he could practically reach out and touch them while he was speaking.

Shortly after they were seated, people began entering—a trickle at first, then a noisy wave as Sunday school let out. The room buzzed with friendly chatter. Though the sanctuary had filled, no one joined Emily and Dorcas on their front-row pew.

At the top of the hour, Dale and Noah entered through the door behind the altar and took their seats on the platform, facing the now-quiet congregation. Noah looked so distractingly handsome in his grey suit, white shirt, and ice-blue tie, she wondered how she would focus on his message.

After the first hymn, Dale stood and crossed to the front of the center aisle to make announcements. Another hymn followed, then the congregation took their seats while Noah took his place behind the pulpit.

Tall and handsome, he gripped the sides of the wooden platform and flashed his million-dollar smile. "Good morning. Pastor Dale was kind enough to allow me to share the Word with you today. We'll be continuing with the study in Corinthians; our text is First Corinthians thirteen, verses four through seven. I'll start with a prayer, and then we'll dig in. Will you pray with me?"

Separated by less than ten feet, Emily sat close enough to detect even the slightest case of nerves in Noah. She saw none. He looked calm and relaxed, completely at home in front of the large crowd. Of course, this modest gathering was nothing for a man who addressed thousands at a Bible study in his home church.

She, on the other hand, was a nervous wreck—sweaty palms and rapid heartbeat—the works. She focused on regulating her breathing. *Please God, help Noah do well. And please don't let me do the weird laughing thing.*

Noah bowed his head. "*Father, we thank You for Your Word. We thank You for the beauty of this familiar passage and ask that You open it to us this morning so that we'll have fresh understanding from You.*"

After the prayer, Noah moved from behind the podium. Not unexpectedly, the man who overflowed with energy walked around while he spoke. He used his arms, his whole body really, to help convey the meaning of his words. Surprisingly, it wasn't distracting.

She was probably biased, but if anything, his movement added life to the message.

Soon she was too caught up in what he was saying to notice what he looked like while he said it. Noah was a natural. His conversational tone and body language invited them to listen, while his well-thought-out message challenged them to think.

He handled the Scriptures with reverence and competence, opening them in a way that encouraged the congregation to apply them. More than once he emphasized that the purpose of studying Scripture was not to gain knowledge, but to walk in obedience to it.

Before she knew it, he finished, and they were on their feet for the closing hymn.

Dorcas nudged her. "I guess I can see why they want him for a television preacher." The singing masked her not-so-quiet whisper. "That boy seems to know what he's about."

Talk about an understatement.

Emily bit back a sigh. The tiny ember of hope burning deep inside her, the silly romantic notion that at this, the eleventh hour, Noah would discover he couldn't live without her and turn his back on his life in Houston, his family heritage, and his brilliant calling to stay with her in Village Green, flickered and died.

Watching him speak, witnessing firsthand his incredible gift, she acknowledged the truth. Noah belonged out there, in front of huge television audiences, where he could make the biggest impact.

She blinked hard to push back looming tears. It had been a silly idea anyway. The practical part of her knew it all along. Men like him didn't end up with women like her.

She and Dorcas chatted with the people standing around them as they slowly made their way down the aisle to the back of the church where Noah and Dale greeted the exiting congregants. Hallie's elderly decorating friend, Mary Jo, invited Emily and Dorcas to join a group of them who were driving to Corsicana for lunch. Emily declined, but Dorcas accepted with delight. Mary Jo assured Emily they would be happy to drive Dorcas home after lunch, a blessing since Emily wanted to spend the time with Noah.

They inched their way to the back of the sanctuary and when their turn to shake Noah's hand finally arrived, Emily suddenly felt shy. This dynamic, beautiful man was destined for greatness. How presumptuous to think she had anything in common with him. How could she ever have thought he would be interested in someone like her?

Dorcas went first, taking Noah's hand and holding it between her gnarled ones while she told him of her lunch plans. Apparently, they'd already said their goodbyes because after reminding him to keep in touch, she gave him a merry wave then trotted off to join Mary Jo.

Last in line, Emily stopped in front of him, her focus trained on his well-polished loafers as she extended her hand.

He took it in both of his. "That bad, huh?"

Surprised, she lifted her face. "Hmmm?"

He kept her hand as his gaze locked with hers. "I depend on you to be honest with me, Doc. The fact you won't look me in the eye says you don't want to tell me my sermon wasn't too good."

Her mouth went slack. He was serious. "Not too good? Noah, you were brilliant." She studied their joined hands. "I confess, I'm more than a little awed by your talent."

"So, you liked it?"

She looked up into his face and slowly shook her head. "No. I don't think *like* is the proper word. I was wowed, Pastor Speers. Absolutely blown away."

"All that?" He smiled, the heart-poundingly familiar smile of her piano-playing companion and friend, reminding her that no matter the chasm separating them, he was still her Noah. "It means a lot to hear it from you."

Dale waved goodbye to a lingering parishioner before turning to them with a broad smile. "Didn't our boy do a great job?" He clapped Noah on the back. "Why don't you two head over to the house while I lock up here? I'll join you in few minutes."

The sun blazed directly overhead as they stepped outside. The air was hot and still, not the slightest breeze to stir it. The last car exited the gravel parking lot onto the street. Noah peeled off his suit jacket and rolled up his shirt sleeves while they followed the sidewalk to the parsonage. They climbed the stairs together, and he unlocked the front door and pushed it open. Cool air and delicious aromas poured out from the house as he signaled her to enter.

She stopped just inside and inhaled deeply. "Something smells delicious."

"Pot roast." He removed his tie and draped it along with his coat on the back of the recliner before leading the way through the living room into the kitchen. "Dale said he wouldn't let me leave until I learned how to make a roast."

Now that she'd witnessed Noah's incredible gift in action, she knew her job was to encourage him to follow God's leading. This wasn't the time to tell him that, pot roast or not, she didn't ever want him to go. "You're definitely leaving here a better cook."

"I'm leaving here a better man." He opened the drawer and selected a handful of silverware. "And I have you and Dale to thank for most of it."

Emily reached into the cabinet for plates. "I know Dale has been teaching you, but I can't imagine what you learned from me."

After they set the table, he surprised her by cupping her face in his palms and brushing a caressing finger over her cheek. "Doc, I've learned so much from you, I'm still trying to sort it all out."

Dale arrived, and the three of them worked to get lunch on the table before settling around it to eat. Emily had little appetite for the delicious meal. Hard to eat when the man who'd come to mean everything to her was leaving. Still, they lingered, talking and laughing as if they weren't aware that precious time ticked away.

Finally, the moment she'd been dreading arrived. Noah placed his napkin on the table beside his plate and glanced at his watch. "As much as I hate to say it, I need to get on the road. I've got a three-hour drive ahead of me, and traffic will be terrible once I get to the outskirts of Houston."

He stood. "Let me get these dishes cleared before I go."

Emily waved him away. "It's my turn to clean up since you two cooked."

Dale nodded. "I'll help her. You do what you need to do."

She and Dale worked side by side in the kitchen while Noah gathered his things and carried them in several loads out to the car.

"We're going to miss him." Dale sighed as he rinsed the plates and placed them in the dishwasher.

Miss him didn't seem strong enough to capture her feelings. "Yeah." Emily nodded as she wrapped leftovers.

The older man shut off the water and turned to her. "You won't abandon me when he's gone, I hope. We make good dinner companions, you and I."

Though she didn't know Dale well enough to know if he preferred his solitude, she knew he'd grown genuinely attached to Noah. She wouldn't be the only one suffering. His leaving would leave a big void in the older man's life as well. She patted him on the back. "Don't worry. You can't get rid of me that easily."

Noah walked into the kitchen, a sheen of perspiration glossing his face and the ends of his carefully styled hair spiking into unruly curls. He'd changed from his suit into a polo shirt and khakis, his version of casual. "That's it. I think I've got it all."

"Let's have a quick prayer before we send you off." The threesome moved to the foyer and held hands while Dale prayed blessings and protection over Noah.

"Amen. And thank you, sir. For everything. I'm grateful for your hospitality, your wisdom, and the cooking lessons. I hope if you're ever in Houston, you'll let me return the favor."

"Maybe one day." Dale's tone indicated he thought the likelihood of him traveling to Houston was remote. He pulled Noah into a hug. "Goodbye, son. It's been wonderful to have you. I'll miss you." He stepped back and, after clearing his throat, turned to her. "Emily, why don't you walk Noah to his car? We've said our goodbyes, so I think I'll stay inside and save my old back from climbing another flight of stairs."

Obviously, he was trying to give them some privacy, although even Dale must have given up on them as a couple. The most optimistic matchmaker in the world couldn't wrangle a happily-ever-after for the two of them. Not when Noah was headed out the door. Forever.

Emily walked beside him down the stairs and to his car. This was it. Goodbye. There were a thousand things she wanted to say to him, but no profound words penetrated the sorrow clouding her mind. "Drive safely. Oh, and Dorcas told me to remind you to keep to the posted speed."

He chuckled. "I can honestly promise to drive slowly, since there's nothing to hurry home to."

Their eyes met and a weighted silence stretched between them. "I'll—"

"I'll—" Emily smiled as they spoke over each other. "You first."

He shrugged. "I was just going to say I'll miss you."

"I'll miss you too."

"I'll miss you more. I'll have no one to force me to eat fried food." He sent her a teasing look.

She planted her hands on her hips. "For the record, I most certainly did not force you to eat anything."

He laughed. "I'll have no one to drop in on unannounced so they can calm me down when I'm entertaining an imagined grievance."

The memories of the times he popped in on her at the clinic brought a smile to her lips.

"I'll have no one to make me take long, painful introspective looks into my heart and motives," he continued. A month in Houston and I'll probably devolve into my old shallow self."

"You aren't shallow."

His smile dimmed. "Who will play duets with me at night and keep me company?"

"I have no doubt you can find any number of people who play piano at least as well as I do." Which didn't make it any less awful to think of someone else sharing a bench and keyboard with him.

"But they won't be you." He took her hand and, gaze locked with hers, raised it to his lips. "Dr. Emily Cutler, there will never be anyone like you."

She promised herself she wouldn't cry in front of him. He had a job to do for the kingdom, and she wouldn't stand in his way. Lowering her gaze to hide the welling tears, she gently disengaged her hand from his and took a step back. "Take care, Noah."

"Goodbye, Emily." He slid his mirrored sunglasses over his eyes and climbed in behind the wheel. With one last long look at her, he swung the door closed and started the car.

She waved as he reversed down the driveway, tears running down her cheeks as he rounded the corner and out of her life.

CHAPTER THIRTEEN

At his cue, Noah strode onto the semicircular stage while the praise team exited from the opposite side. The technicians killed the lights over the musicians' area, burying the abandoned instruments in shadows, and dimmed the lights in the massive auditorium. Two bright spots shone on the Plexiglas podium.

TV cameras followed Noah as he moved into the light, his smiling face projected onto giant screens mounted to the right and left of the stage. He lifted a hand in greeting to the thousands of strangers. "Good morning, church. I've got a lot to share with you today, so let's pray, and we'll dive right in."

After leading the congregation in prayer, he picked up his Bible and stepped away from the podium. "This morning we're going to continue our study in Isaiah." He flipped open to the text and slid in a finger to hold his page. "Before I begin with today's passage, I want to give us some background information to establish context. We want to be sure we are reading and understanding Scripture as it was intended, rather than using it to promote our own agendas."

Thirty-two minutes later, as documented by the countdown clock prominently posted on the opposite wall, he closed in prayer and exited the stage while the house lights and prerecorded music came up, and slick announcements scrolled across the twin screens where his face had been seconds earlier. As he stepped behind the curtain, one of the production team removed his microphone headset while another collected the battery pack from his belt.

His father met him on the other side of the soundproofed door. "Nice job, Noah. Don't know that I could do better myself."

"Thank you." They walked side by side down the hall to the executive lounge. Noah pushed open the door and signaled his father to enter ahead of him.

"Powerful word this morning, Pastor Noah." His assistant waited inside to hand him a chilled bottle of water.

Noah accepted it, twisted off the cap, and drank deeply. "Thanks, Bill."

"My pleasure." The middle-aged man clutched his ever-present clipboard to his chest. "Can I get you anything before I go?"

Noah shook his head. "Not for me. Dad, do you need anything?"

"No. I'm good."

Bill nodded. "Okay. Pastor Noah, I'll be back to get you in forty-five minutes for the second service. If you need something before then, don't hesitate to call." He pointed to the phone next to the arrangement of fresh flowers on the coffee table before moving soundlessly over the thick carpet and stepping out into the hall.

"Thanks, man." Noah waved his gratitude. "Appreciate it."

"Your grandfather and I were talking about this series you're doing." His father settled onto the corner of the long gray modular sofa that bordered two walls. "We're impressed. And we're not the only ones. Viewership continues to grow each week. Last week we had twenty-five thousand households for the eleven o'clock service."

Noah shrugged out of his suit coat and draped it over the back of the couch. He took another long swallow of his water before sitting beside his dad. "That's great."

His father studied him a moment, then frowned. "You don't sound impressed. Let me put it another way. That's at least twenty-five thousand people who weren't in church and yet heard the gospel. Technology is an amazing tool for the kingdom."

Noah nodded, absently picking at the paper label on the bottle. He wanted to be excited, certainly he rejoiced the gospel was going out, but honestly, he felt disconnected from the television viewers. He didn't know these people. Didn't know their stories. He battled the same feeling of separation as he'd addressed the crowd gathered here in the stadium seating. Worse, he felt distant from God.

He eased back into the cushions, allowing his gaze to track around the plush room reserved exclusively for use by the pastoral staff or guest speakers. The lounge served as a peaceful haven to shut out distractions and allow the user to focus on God while mentally preparing for the service. Funny that even with its tastefully muted colors and expertly arranged furniture, the professionally designed space wasn't half as peaceful and conducive to finding God as that old bare-bones church in Village Green.

Noah gave himself a mental shake. What was the matter with him? His prayers had finally been answered. He was teaching God's Word at the largest church in the South. He was operating in his gift, living his best life.

So where was the satisfaction? The joy?

After an expectant pause, his father stood. "It's clear you've got the next service on your mind, so I'll run along and give you some quiet." He walked toward the door. "Your mother told me to remind you she's expecting you for lunch. She's taken it in her head that you're losing weight, so we're having all your favorite foods to tempt you." He grinned before putting a finger to his lips. "Don't tell her I told you."

Noah chuckled. "I won't. Tell her I'll be there as soon as I finish here."

"Good enough. See you in a bit."

In no time at all, Bill tapped lightly on the door before poking his head in. "You're on in five, Pastor Noah."

He pushed himself off the sofa with new determination. Time to get his head back in the game, to move forward and embrace his God-given calling. After sliding on his suit jacket and checking his appearance in the lighted mirror in the dressing room, he gathered his Bible and headed back down the hall to the auditorium. Two technicians met him behind the curtains and wired him for sound. At his cue, he put a smile on his face and strode back out onto the stage.

Noah pulled up into his parents' circular driveway and parked behind his grandfather's Mercedes. September heat rose off the pavestones as he crossed to the house and let himself in.

Though not quite a palace, his childhood home fit in nicely with the surrounding mansions in the tony neighborhood. His father pulled down a hefty salary from the church, but it was oil money from his mother's side of the family that supported the lavish lifestyle he'd known all his life.

A rush of cool air greeted him as he stepped over the threshold and slipped off his sunglasses. "Anybody home?"

"Oh good, you're here." His mother, still a beautiful woman in her sixties, bustled in and enveloped him in a perfumed hug. "We're at the table, visiting."

He followed her along gleaming marble floors past the elegantly appointed formal living room and an equally elegant dining room featuring a mahogany table long enough to seat twenty, to the sunroom where she liked to entertain smaller parties. Bordered on three sides by spotless glass walls and overlooking the well-maintained grounds and pool, the dome-ceilinged sunroom held a circular table that seated six.

His father and grandfather stood as they entered. "Here's our guest of honor now."

His grandfather stepped forward and wrapped him in a bear hug. "I watched the second service on television. My boy, I don't think I'm being biased when I say your preaching improves every week."

"Thank you, sir."

The older man pulled back to look at him, while keeping an affectionate arm framed around Noah's shoulders. "You were a fine speaker before, but you're fine-tuning your skills to perfection. I'm very proud of you."

"I picked up some tips from your buddy, Dale." In fact, Dale promised to record the services so he and Noah could talk about them later.

Watching Dale relate so effectively to his congregation had been an education to Noah and he'd soaked it up like a sponge. The older man's style was simple, clean, and fresh. No shouting. No theatrics. Just truth. Dale trusted that his congregation had the maturity to handle the whole Word, made his points with clear authority, and let the Scripture take top billing.

It pleased and surprised him that his grandfather found his sermon praiseworthy, since the depth of content and delivery he'd adopted since his trip to Village Green were so different from his father's and grandfather's. He knew both men loved God and served Him as they'd been gifted. Dale said it best when he said ministry wasn't a one-size-fits-all proposition. Plenty of room for variety in the kingdom.

"Come, sit down," his mother said. "Mrs. Bilardi is ready to serve."

Noah took the seat next to his grandfather. The round table was meticulously set with fine china and gleaming crystal, and covered with several linen cloths, artfully layered so their complementary shades were visible. A large yet tasteful arrangement of fresh flowers sat in the center.

As he smoothed his napkin in his lap, the family cook arrived, pushing their lunches on a stainless-steel cart. She moved around the table, placing a plate of fresh greens topped with perfectly seared ahi tuna on the silver charger in front of each of them. A separate footed dish held a colorful fruit salad.

"This looks delicious, Mrs. Bilardi," Noah said as she set a cruet of vinaigrette beside his plate. He glanced at the lavish meal. "It must have taken you hours to make all this."

She blinked in surprise. "Yes, it did. And it was my pleasure." She beamed at him. "It's nice to have you home, Mr. Noah."

"Thank you. I'm . . . uh . . . it's great to see everyone." He couldn't honestly answer he was glad to be home, because he wasn't. *Yet.* Since pulling into town a month ago, he'd been stalled out in a semi-funk.

A lifelong Houstonian, his hometown had become unfamiliar in his absence. The constant noise and heavy traffic annoyed him, his friends seemed shallow and obnoxiously urbane, and the church where he would spend his next forty years was as warm and inviting as a shopping mall.

And speaking of shopping malls, when had they become over-bright, overcrowded glass- and-steel monstrosities stuffed with junk nobody needed?

Since the traffic, friends, stores, and shoppers hadn't changed, the problem was obviously with him. He wasn't the same person who left town just weeks ago. He reassured himself that his dissatisfaction with everything Houston and his fast-paced life would be short-lived. After spending time in Podunk, it would take a while to regain his footing in the city. He likened it to coming up too fast after a dive and getting the bends.

Admittedly, the adjustment was taking longer than expected.

Once everyone was served, his father said, "Dad, why don't you say grace?"

They bowed their heads as his grandfather prayed for God's blessing on the food and on Noah's ministry.

"I saw Sheridan the other day." His mother smiled at Noah over the napkin-lined basket of Mrs. Bilardi's homemade yeast rolls as she placed it in his hands. "She said she'd been over to visit you."

He accepted the basket, helped himself to a serving, and passed it to his grandfather. "That's right. She stopped by the office two weeks ago. She wanted to talk about her singles group." *And hint that it was time to do something about the fact they were both single.*

"She's a lovely young woman. So intelligent. So poised and gracious. And she comes from such a good family."

No mistaking where she was going with the conversation. Sheridan was everything he'd been raised to look for in a wife. With their shared upbringing, experiences, and social circle, she would make a wonderful hostess and an asset to his ministry. The realization had passed through his mind as she'd sat in his office that morning. He could visualize her standing at his side at church and civic events. But he couldn't see her ministering to "the least of these" or volunteering to eat lunch with an old woman with a potty mouth and a penchant for picking her teeth. Sheridan was perfect. But not for him.

Noah nodded agreeably. "She's great."

His grandfather caught his eye and winked. "Noah tells me he met a special woman while he was in Village Green."

"The doctor?" His mother's face puckered like she'd caught a whiff of something unpleasant. "Yes, he's mentioned her."

Noah hadn't planned to bring up Emily to the family, but he couldn't seem to help himself. He missed her, and everything reminded him of her. Talking about her made her feel closer.

"He's known her such a short time." The implication of her dismissive remark being easy come, easy go. She must have noted the displeasure on Noah's face because she added, "Though she sounds very attractive."

"She's beautiful. And really smart." He thought about the quiet insight Emily brought to every conversation. "Maybe brilliant."

"How smart can she be if she ended up in a remote place like that?" His mother trilled a little laugh. "I'm sure she's very nice, but I imagine the brilliant candidates end up in the larger, more prestigious positions."

As Noah buttered his still-warm roll, he wondered if Mrs. Bilardi would teach him how to make them. He bet Dale would get a kick out of making bread, especially if it involved digging into squishy dough up to his elbows.

He turned to his mother and smiled. "Do you know, I said almost the same thing to Emily over lunch one day. As though working in a metropolitan area somehow made a person superior."

Her mouth turned down. "I wasn't suggesting that."

"I asked her why she wasted her talent there. Surely a woman with her skills wanted to do something significant with her life." The remembered words grated on his conscience. Emily must have thought he was such a snob. "Lucky for me, she's as gracious as she is wise and didn't take offense at my clearly offensive question. She told me she was right where God wanted her to be, and because she was in His will, even the smallest thing she did was significant."

His grandfather nodded. "I like the way that young woman thinks."

"She sounds very nice," his mother allowed. "And certainly, small towns need doctors too."

"And preachers." Noah turned to his dad. Dale's predicament had been in the forefront of his mind since he returned home. "Speaking of which, have you had any success finding candidates to send to the pulpit committee in Village Green?"

Lowering his fork, he shook his head. "Not so far. Honestly, finding someone to take the pastorate in such a small church is tough. The salary they're offering is low, even with the value of living in a parsonage factored in."

Noah nodded.

"Young people just starting out in ministry need more than that to live on and support their families," his grandfather said. "Older people don't want the responsibility of running a church, even a small one, without support staff. They've reached the stage in life where they've earned some ease."

"I know you're right. But it's such a great little church. I hate to think of them closing their doors because no one will take it."

"I haven't given up. I suggested to the committee that they consider becoming a two-point charge. They could partner with another small church in the area and share the expense of a pastor. They would need to stagger worship times, say one at nine thirty and the next at eleven, and the pastor could preach at one and have enough time to get to the next. Rural areas do that all the time."

Noah thought about all the lonely widows Dale checked on every week. "But how would one person see to the needs of both congregations? I know from experience visitation in Village Green is a full-time job."

"They'll definitely have to make some sacrifices." The older man shrugged philosophically before scooping up another bite of fish. "That's reality, Son."

Emily Cutler did not mope.

Moping was for unimaginative people who didn't know how to trust God with their lives.

It may have looked like moping, the way her shoulders drooped just a bit, or the slight delay before she could produce a creditable smile, but it wasn't. Because Emily Cutler didn't mope.

Her untouched lunch spread out in front of her on a napkin, she propped her elbows on her desk, sank her chin into her hands, and sighed. She glanced around her newly refurbished office, knowing the pretty cream-colored walls, new-to-her furniture, and plush rug under her feet should brighten her mood. And it did. To a point.

It was just that her spirits were so low, the boost from her now-beautiful office could only push her from morose to mildly depressed.

If she were one of her patients, she would prescribe sunshine and exercise, healthy eating, and spending intentional time with friends—all excellent strategies to ward off the blues. Knowing them to be efficacious, she diligently applied the steps to her own life.

In the morning before work, she made several brisk passes around the Green before showering and dressing for the day. Even in the October heat, she sat outside in the sun for five minutes during her lunch hour. On weekends she played softball, joined a Sunday school class, and accepted invitations to lunch or dinner with whoever was going. Hallie and Trey had her over for dinner twice, and this past weekend, she'd reciprocated.

She was taking care of her body and spending time with friends.

Unfortunately, as nice as all her acquaintances were and as much fun as they had together, they weren't Noah.

She missed Noah.

She'd warned herself he'd be trouble. She'd told herself to keep him at arm's length. To enjoy his company with the knowledge it was only temporary. Not to get attached.

She'd done it anyway.

Despite the sure knowledge he would break her heart, she'd given it to him. And now he was gone.

Nothing felt right since he left. The sunshine seemed tarnished, the insect sounds at night were mournful, and softball was just a game. Food lost its taste, work served only to pay the bills, and gathering with friends reminded her of just how lonely she was.

Talking with him helped.

They'd agreed to keep in touch when he left, but realistically she hadn't expected much. He'd said he'd call, and because he was a man of his word, she knew he would. The problem was, she couldn't hope to compete with his full calendar of business and social commitments. However noble his intentions, the calls would inevitably grow shorter and more infrequent, finally dwindling to nothing as he moved into his exciting future. It was naive to think the sweetness of what they'd shared could withstand the pressures of the real world.

Even as the depressing thought wended through her mind, a smile tugged at her lips. Time and distance were formidable enemies, but they hadn't won yet. Noah had surprised her by calling just to chat—not once, but twice—on his trip back to Houston. Since then, they texted multiple times a day and spoke on the phone for hours at night. They talked about important things, like work and spiritual insights, and insignificant things like what they'd eaten for dinner. To Emily the topic wasn't as important as hearing his voice.

The calls had fallen into a kind of pattern. They'd talk and laugh together, just like they did when they'd shared a piano bench. Some comment would spark the reminder that they were separated, and the conversation would drift to a weighted silence. He'd sigh. She'd sigh.

He'd tell her he missed her. She'd tell him she missed him. He'd sigh. She'd sigh.

He'd tell her he wished they were together. She'd tell him she wished they could be together. More sighs. More silence.

A hopeless situation.

Because they both acknowledged there was no time, even the distant future, when their commitments and circumstances would change and allow them to be together, neither ventured into deep discussions of heart matters. It seemed cruel to introduce longings that would never be satisfied. Their relationship was a dead end. By unspoken agreement, their tenderest emotions remained locked up in their own hearts.

Emily loved Noah. She'd suspected it when he was in Village Green, but really, having the attention of a perfect specimen of manhood made it difficult to think clearly. In her flattered inexperience, she might have been mistaking infatuation for love.

With the passage of time came a settled certainty. She loved him.

She might be new to the whole male/female relationship thing, but she recognized what she felt for him was the real deal. Attraction, certainly, but beyond that, an abiding affection and respect. Love. And with that love came the determination she would never do anything to derail God's plan and mission for Noah. To love someone meant to want the very best for them. The man she loved was destined for greatness. She would do everything in her power to stay out of the way.

So, she prayed. She prayed God would bless and guide Noah. She asked that His perfect will would be accomplished in Noah's life.

She prayed for herself, that she would be satisfied with their long-distance friendship for as long as it lasted. She asked for peace and joy in the days ahead as God guided her along the path he had chosen for her.

She also prayed for the strength to wholeheartedly support Noah's ministry. To celebrate his success without begrudging the cost to herself.

Finally, because she knew Noah cared deeply for her, she asked God to put a guard on her tongue so she would never say anything to make him want to sacrifice his calling for a future with her.

A glance at the clock told her she had fifteen minutes before her next patient. If she planned to eat, it needed to be now. Emily picked up her peanut butter sandwich and took a bite. She grimaced as she chewed. Her lunchtime favorite tasted dry and bland, much like her life without Noah.

Emily carried a load of dishes to the sink. "Dinner was delicious, Dale."

He followed close behind her with their glasses. "I've never cooked with fennel before. I'm glad it turned out. I commend you for your bravery in agreeing to sample these new recipes I've found on the internet. It's always nice to have medical personnel on site if anything were to go wrong."

She laughed as she rinsed the plates and placed them in the

dishwasher. "It was delicious, as they've all been. You're a wonderful cook. Thank you for inviting me."

"I should be the one thanking you." He stood on the other side of the dishwasher and fitted the glasses into the top rack. "I have agreeable company for dinner *and* help with the cleanup."

She knew Dale missed Noah almost as much as she did. Since he left two months ago, she and the pastor met weekly for dinner, friendship, and conversation. They bonded over their mutual loss. Both communicated regularly with Noah and frequently their discussions over dinner were based on those conversations.

Because Dale was a good friend and she knew she could trust him with her secrets, she confided to him the words she would never tell another soul. She loved Noah. Not only did she love him now, but she feared she always would.

"Do you want to run over to the church and play the piano?" he asked after they'd cleaned up the kitchen. "I won't be able to sit with you. I've got a few things to catch up on in the office tonight."

"Sure." They'd established a comfortable routine on their evenings together. After they ate the meal Dale had prepared and the dessert she'd picked up from the bakery, they would walk over to the church so she could play the piano. Sometimes he stayed to listen, while other times he worked in the office, but when they were finished, he escorted her back to her car.

The last remnants of sunlight painted the sky a deep red as they made their way from the parsonage. From the corner of her eye, she noted her elderly patient moved with a natural gait. Thank goodness he appeared to have recovered fully from his back injury. He unlocked the front door of the church, disarmed the security system, and turned on the overhead lights in the sanctuary. They walked the center aisle together and when she took a left toward the piano, he veered right around the altar to the door behind it.

"Enjoy your music, Emily dear," he said with a wave. "If you finish first, come find me and we'll walk home together."

Emily scooped up a hymnal from the lectern and seated herself on the bench at the baby grand. After switching on the reading light, she positioned the hymnal on the shelf just so and sat back with a sigh.

Playing the piano had taken on new meaning since Noah left. The old hobby still ministered to the deepest places in her soul, but in addition, now the melodies stirred memories of the sweet times they'd shared.

Sitting here, side by side, they'd become acquainted. In this sacred corner they'd shared laughs and songs and stories. On this bench, they crossed a seemingly impassable chasm as Beauty and the Beast and made the unexpected transition from casual acquaintances to genuine friends.

On this very spot, she'd fallen in love.

Emily blew out a breath. This sort of thinking was not helpful. She should be focusing on the future, not languishing in the past. She flipped open the hymnal and turned to "A Mighty Fortress is Our God." Without Noah to handle the bass clef, she'd had to play both hands by herself. With practice she could manage it, but it wasn't the same.

As her fingers found the notes, she had a feeling that would be true in her life. Meeting Noah changed everything. Sharing the keyboard with him had made the song better. Richer. Sharing her days with him made her life better. Richer.

With practice she could live without him, but it wouldn't be the same.

When the last notes drifted off, she turned to "What a Friend We Have in Jesus." Maybe the old favorite would bolster her sagging spirits.

Tears welled as she played through the first stanza. After the second verse, when they were so thick she couldn't see the printed page, she reverted to the piece she knew from memory. "Be Thou My Vision."

Eyes closed, tears streaming down her cheeks, she played the song as a heartfelt prayer. She lifted her face heavenward. *Father, I trust You. But this is so hard. Give me clarity to see Your path. Show me the way to find joy in Your plan.*

Noah had particularly enjoyed this hymn. He'd sit beside her, hip to hip, to listen to her play. Tonight, as the music filled the sanctuary, she could almost feel his warmth. She breathed deeply. Her imagination stretched until she could actually smell his cologne.

Her fingers paused on the keys as the sophisticated clean smell scented the air. Nobody's imagination was *that* good. She opened her eyes and turned her head to the left.

"Noah?" She hopped off the bench and threw herself into his arms. "You're here!"

He laughed as he drew her close. "I wanted to surprise you."

He was so warm, so solid, so Noah, she didn't want to let go. She buried her face against his chest, her tears dampening the front of his once-crisp shirt.

Still encircling her with his arms, he arched back to look down into her face. "What's the matter?"

"Nothing." She sniffled. "I've just missed you, that's all."

"Aw, Doc." He gently swiped at the moisture with the pads of his thumbs. "I've missed you too."

She studied him through damp lashes, reacquainting herself with every inch of his beloved face. "You're here. I can't believe you're really here." After a moment, she frowned. "Why are you here?"

His expression grew serious. "I needed to talk to you."

Emily's heart stuttered with apprehension. They spoke on the phone every day. What was so important that he needed to say it to her face? She stepped back from his arms. "Okay."

He sat on the bench and pointed to the spot she'd just vacated. "Come sit next to me."

Her eyes remained trained on his as she lowered herself beside him.

Face grim, he took her hand in his. "This distance thing isn't working."

Her breath caught while she managed a slow nod.

"We're wasting precious time."

She dropped her gaze to their joined hands.

"What would you think about me taking Dale's place?"

A buzzing started in her brain. Her brows knit as she tried to process his question. "Here? You'd come here? To Village Green?"

Smiling, he nodded.

"As the pastor?" She tried to think over the static in her head. "Did the committee offer you the job?"

His movie-star smile spread as he nodded again.

She told herself the flush on his handsome face was pleasure, but one of them was obviously delirious. She placed a hand on her forehead, then transferred it to his. Both cool. No fever. "Why?"

He lifted his shoulders in an easy shrug. "Because they need a pastor." He looked down into her eyes. "And I need you."

He needed her? Every one of her internal organs went to mush. *He needed her.* Were there any more beautiful words in the English language?

She blinked. *Wait.* What was she doing? Hadn't she promised God she wouldn't do anything to stand in the way of God's plans for Noah? "No. Absolutely not."

Surprised, he rocked back. "No? You don't want me to take the job?"

She shook her head while simultaneously begging God for the strength to stand firm. "No. You can't." She gathered his hands into hers and looked into his eyes. "You are the most gifted man I've ever known. Truly, Noah, you have an incredible ability to teach Scripture in ways people can understand. You are destined for great things."

She took a deep breath, fortifying herself to speak her convictions even though the words were guaranteed to break her heart. "I am so honored you want to be with me, but I couldn't live with myself if you buried yourself in Village Green and wasted your talent."

His expression softened. "A wise woman once told me she didn't measure success by the size of her ministry but by whether or not she was in the center of God's will."

Hope flickered. "Yes, but . . . that's true, but . . . what about your commitments to your church? To your family?"

"They released me."

She gave him a side-eyed glance. "Just like that?"

He chuckled. "No. It took a lot of discussion, and my mom cried for a week, but after they had time to pray and consider it, they agreed I should go where God leads."

"Don't I remember you saying Village Green would never be God's will for you?"

"Many times. It appears the Almighty has a sense of humor."

She searched his face, looking for reassurance. "And you're sure this is where God is leading?"

"Without a doubt."

It was difficult to form a rational thought with him looking at her like that and his palm tenderly cupping her cheek. "Who'll take your dad's place as head pastor?"

"Nobody for now. He's healthy. Realistically, he's probably got another fifteen or twenty good years of preaching left in him."

Practical Emily refused to give way to joy until her understanding was complete. "So . . . you're just walking away."

"Not exactly. And that's one of the things I wanted to talk about with you. I want to take the pastorate here. But Dad's church has asked me to do an online Bible study series for them, which would involve me going to Houston once a month to record a month's worth of lessons. What do you think—"

She pounced on the solution. "Yes!"

He grinned. "Sounds like you're agreeable."

"Noah, having you here with me would be the answer to my every prayer. But as selfish as I am, I don't want others to miss your gift. Thousands of people would have access to your online study, right?"

He tilted his head in consideration for a moment, then nodded.

"So, you'll be fulfilling your calling. And the part of me that's afraid you'll be miserable after a month of living in Village Green is relieved you'll have a regularly scheduled monthly trip back to the big city that will give you something to look forward to. You could go to all the restaurants and stores you won't have access to here."

"You'd be surprised at how unappealing that sounds. Unless you'll go with me."

"I will." Practical considerations satisfied, she allowed the rush of joy to flood her. She and Noah would be together. A thought intruded on her delight, and she frowned. "Do your parents hate me?"

He laughed. "They love you because I do. And they're eager to meet you. I told them I'd bring you back for the weekend, if you're free."

He loved her? "What did you say?"

"I said my parents are eager to meet you—"

Emily shook her head. "No, the other part. About them loving me because you do."

He smiled tenderly. "I do love you. I think I started falling in love with you the second time we were together."

Not the first time, certainly, since she spent the evening laughing at him.

"I didn't tell you before because sensible people don't fall in love in a week or two. And even when I knew it was love, I didn't tell you because I didn't see any way for us to be together. You deserve someone who can be here with you."

"I don't want anyone else. I love you, Noah. Only you."

His face lit with a look of endearing wonder. "You do? I hoped so. I prayed so."

She nodded. "I love you very much."

"That brings me to my second question. Will you marry me?"

"Yes. Oh yes. Absolutely."

His dark eyes danced as he raised her hand to his lips and their gazes met over their joined hands. "I have one final question for you, Doc."

"Hmmm?"

"May I kiss you?"

"I thought you'd never ask."

She lifted her face to his, her eyes fluttering shut as his lips met hers. The soft pressure of his mouth caused delicious stirrings, and she hummed with pleasure. With an answering sigh, he slid his arms around her, pulling her close and deepening the kiss.

Wow. Good thing she was sitting down.

"Oh ho!" Dale called from the now-open doorway behind the altar. "From the looks of things, she must have said yes."

They split apart with guilty haste.

"You knew?" Emily's head swiveled from one man to the other. "He knew?"

Noah nodded. "He's been my spiritual and romantic adviser from the beginning."

They stood and walked hand in hand to the middle aisle to join Dale.

"Congratulations. I see a bright future for you and the church." The older man had tears in his eyes as he hugged them. "Now that Noah's here to walk you back to your car, I believe I'll head on to the house. Good night, Emily. Noah, your room is ready for you. I'll leave the door unlocked." With a smile and a wave, Dale strode down the aisle.

Emily felt a sad tug at her heart as she watched him depart. She and Noah weren't the only ones whose lives were about to be changed dramatically. When she heard the outer door close, she turned to Noah. "What will happen to him once you replace him? A man as active as Dale will waste away without something meaningful to do."

"I agree. That's why I've asked him to continue on as my mentor." He reached over to take her hand. "And if it's okay with you, I'd like him to stay in the parsonage once we're married. We can find someplace else to live. I don't want to drive him from his home."

Once we're married. Tears welled again. Happy tears. In the course of an hour, she'd gone from lonely desolation to an offer of marriage from the most wonderful man she'd ever known. Sometimes the goodness of God overwhelmed her. "My apartment is beautiful and plenty big for the two of us."

He studied her face. "You don't mind?"

"Not at all. It's a thoughtful and wise solution." She smiled into his handsome face. "Exactly what I would expect from the man I love."

Noah pulled Emily close, reveling in the pure pleasure of holding her in his arms. What had he done to deserve the love of this wonderful woman?

A wave of joy and anticipation, underscored with soul-deep contentment, rolled over him. He scanned the small sanctuary with its hundred-year-old stained glass windows and scarred wooden pews. By the grace of God, this sacred old space would be his home. He lifted his face in silent prayer to the One who brought him to this woman, this place. *Thank You.*

Noah rested his cheek on the top of her head. "I love you, Emily. I don't deserve you, but I promise to spend the rest of my life becoming a man worthy of you."

She eased back in the circle of his arms to turn her eyes to his. "I think you're perfect just the way you are."

"One of the many reasons why I love you." And because he did, he kissed her again.

Emily sighed. "I feel like I'm dreaming." Her expression grew serious. "I need to ask you one more time. Are you absolutely sure about this? About me and Village Green?"

Gently, he cupped her face with his hands and tipped it up so their eyes held. "Doc, I've never been so sure of anything in my life. We're in this together. Forever. Heart and soul."

www.ingramcontent.com/pod-product-compliance
Lightning Source LLC
Chambersburg PA
CBHW051132020726
47501CB00005B/1471